THE ELUSIVE DOCTOR

Wearing spectacles to make herself appear more dignified, twenty-year-old Candy gained the longed-for post as secretary to the two principals of a school in the African mountains. She was often overworked, sometimes shocked, occasionally unhappy. But all through her days at the school there ran a single thread, which bound her to the one person with whom she felt most at ease, the man who finally said unforgivable, hurtful things — the man she could not forget.

Books by Claire Vernon
in the Linford Romance Library:

THE DOCTOR WAS A DOLL

CLAIRE VERNON

THE ELUSIVE DOCTOR

Complete and Unabridged

LINFORD
Leicester

First published in Great Britain

First Linford Edition
published 1999

British Library CIP Data

Vernon, Claire, *1906* –
 The elusive doctor.—Large print ed.—
 Linford romance library
 1. Love stories
 2. Large type books
 I. Title
 823.9'14 [F]

 ISBN 0–7089–5513–4

Published by
F. A. Thorpe (Publishing) Ltd.
Anstey, Leicestershire

Set by Words & Graphics Ltd.
Anstey, Leicestershire
Printed and bound in Great Britain by
T. J. International Ltd., Padstow, Cornwall

This book is printed on acid-free paper

1

A Different World

There had been four girls originally waiting in that cool, impersonal hotel room. Now there was only Candy, still waiting to be interviewed.

She sat, uncomfortably nervous, a slight girl with huge grey eyes half-hidden by the large ugly spectacles, her hand tugging nervously at her white gloves. Outside the hotel, the African sun was blazing down and it was hard to realise that, only a few days before, she had been in London and in the middle of a bitterly cold winter.

The door opened and Dr. Faulkner stood in the doorway, frowning a little as Candy got hastily to her feet. He towered above her, a heavily-built man, handsome, with dark, deep-set eyes and a very pleasant voice. She followed him into the room, sat down as directed and folded her hands demurely in her lap as the tall man in the dark tropical-weight suit and grey silk tie took his place behind the desk. He was younger than she had first thought, probably in his mid-thirties, and was the headmaster of a co-educational school, and she hoped she was going to be his secretary.

He returned her curious gaze and she felt rather uncomfortable and, for once, lacked self-confidence. She felt unlike herself. Indeed, she *looked* very unlike herself!

When her mother had read out the advertisement for the job, she had chuckled and said: 'A woman of dignified appearance, Candy. I'm sure he won't expect a flippant bit of a girl with a tip-tilted nose and such wild dark curls.'

That was logic so Candy had carefully *disguised* herself. Now, as she nervously jerked the heavy horn-rimmed spectacles back up her small nose, she hoped he would not guess the lens were made of plain glass! She had bought them only that morning, and the demure navy-blue shantung suit as well for this occasion. She had disciplined her wild hair. At least she hoped so! She had brushed and strained it back firmly from her face and neck and twisted it into a small chignon on top of her head. Only somehow she had an allergy or something for hairpins and they kept falling out and she was terrified lest the whole thing collapse before the interview was over. In addition she had discarded her usual spindle-heeled shoes for sensible low-heeled ones, and hoped the white straw hat made a dignified crown to the whole outfit. She had thought she looked much older and more dignified but now as Dr. Faulkner studied her, she began to doubt it.

'I understand you have just come to Africa from England,' he asked now in his deep attractive voice.

'Yes, my mother came out for . . . '

She stopped just in time! She had nearly betrayed the fact that she only wanted the job for six months! 'She has come out to work here and . . . and brought me with her. We planned to take a flat in Durban but now she finds she has to move about between here, Johannesburg and Cape Town and so . . . so I am looking for a living-in post.'

There was no need to tell him of their bitter disappointment nor of Candy's dislike of going to the 'Y' which might be very nice but was a poor substitute for a flat of their own.

He offered her a cigarette and when she refused, said in a surprised voice: 'You don't smoke?'

'Oh, yes, I do smoke,' Candy admitted honestly. 'But my mother says you should not smoke at an interview.'

He coughed suddenly and it was a moment or two before he could start asking questions again. 'Your name is . . . ' He was looking at the form she had completed.

'Candace White,' Candy said quickly. No need to tell him that she had been called Candy since the day of her birth! 'I worked for Professor Scrivener at the London University,' she went on quickly. 'For — for nearly two years. I have a reference . . . ' She opened her handbag, confused, because she realised she should have pinned the reference to the application form.

'Don't bother,' Dr. Faulkner said rather coolly.

She closed her handbag and her heart sank — for that could only mean she had no chance. She looked round the air-conditioned gilt and white room. *How* could she make him give her the job? She would work so hard . . .

Dr. Faulkner picked up the thick horn-rimmed glasses that lay on the desk and began twirling them. 'You are very young . . . '

She had expected this. She lifted her chin. 'I am nearly twenty-two . . . '

Her cheeks burned with angry shame

as she saw him glance at the application form and then glance at her, his eyebrows lifted. 'I see that you are twenty-one years old and two weeks exactly . . . ' he said very gently.

There was an endless — a terrible silence. 'Yes, I am,' she said very meekly. 'But girls mature far earlier than men do, you know . . . ' she added eagerly.

Was that a twinkle in his eyes? 'Do they?' he asked.

'Oh yes . . . ' Candy began and took a deep breath. 'Mummy has taught me to be very conscientious and I would work very hard . . . ' She stopped, appalled by her rush of breathless words. Was this *dignified behaviour*?

He spoke slowly. 'My sister and I require a secretary to handle our voluminous correspondence, to deal with the ledgers and accounts, and also handle difficult parents. That is why we require an older, more sophisticated woman.' He twirled his glasses and looked at her. 'You would miss London.'

'Perhaps but . . . but I love the country,' she told him eagerly.

He smiled. 'This is . . . well, this is much more than mere country, and it is very isolated. Why do you want the job so badly?'

She jerked her glasses back up her nose and leaned forward eagerly.

'Because . . . because . . . you see, Mummy will be away lecturing all the time and I just hate the thought of going to the 'Y' and . . . '

'Your mother lectures?' he asked, showing little interest and giving Candy the feeling that he was merely postponing the evil moment when he must tell her that she could not have the job, that she was too young, etc. etc.

'Yes, she is Dr. Elisa White,' Candy said and could not hide the pride in her voice. 'She is a children's specialist and has been asked out here to lecture and teach her treatment for spastic children.'

That interested him! He leaned forward, his face alight with interest.

'Is she *the* Dr. Elisa White?' he asked.

Candy nodded and smiled. 'Yes. She lectures all over the world. Everyone knows my mother,' she said very proudly.

'I most certainly have heard of her,' Dr. Faulkner said and she saw that he was impressed. 'Are you her only child?'

'Yes but I always think it is a shame she only had me,' Candy told him in her young eager voice. 'She ought to have been like the 'Old Woman who lived in a Shoe', only my mother would have known what to do for she is wonderful with children.'

Dr. Faulkner unexpectedly chuckled and looked suddenly much younger.

'Perhaps the rest of the world would have suffered for she wouldn't have had time for the other children,' he suggested.

'Oh, she would have,' Candy told

him very earnestly. 'She would have *made* time. Mummy always says that if you really want to do a thing, you'll make time to do it. Otherwise it is just an excuse to wriggle out of doing something you don't really want to do . . . ' Candy paused for breath, a little dismayed by her own talkativeness.

There was a sudden silence as he doodled on the handsome blotter before him. Then he looked up and began to talk about the school — that he and his sister ran it, that they had great plans for future developments. It was all a little above Candy's head and she felt her mother would have been more interested but she kept still and tried very hard to look intelligent. He showed her photographs of the school, an impressive-looking large building, partly covered by creepers. And then he said — oh, so casually:

'You would not have to work with the children, except perhaps escort a child to the dentist . . . '

He went on to talk about salaries, her time off, the holidays but Candy heard it from a great distance for she was tense with excitement and fear she had misunderstood him — in case she had read too much into casual words. But then he said — and this settled it. 'You would work for my sister and myself but would eat with the staff and share their social life . . . '

So it was true? She was getting the job! She felt limp with excitement and she heard the arrangements he was making for her as from a long distance. In four days' time, the school car would pick her up at the hotel.

Oh, it was all too wonderful for words. It all fitted in so perfectly for that was the day her mother had to fly to Cape Town.

Somehow she spoke lucidly, shook hands with him, left the room and floated along the hot crowded streets to the hotel; sat on the small balcony gazing at the incredibly blue sea as she waited impatiently until her mother arrived and then flung herself at the tall, white-haired woman with blue eyes and absurdly youthful face.

'I've got it, Mummy . . . I've got it.'

Later they sat together on the balcony, revelling in the sunshine, watching the swimmers in the blue sea, the people sun-bathing on the golden sands, and talked together, wondering again at the way their lives had changed.

'Just think, Mummy . . . ' Candy cried excitedly. 'Less than six weeks ago, I battled home from work through that vile yellow fog and you came home with the news that we were coming out here for six months.' She stretched luxuriously in the warm sunshine. 'And here we are — isn't it all wonderful?'

'Wonderful, indeed.' Her mother sighed happily. 'Some of the doctors I met today were so nice, Candy,' she said dreamily in a way quite unlike her. 'One especially — an American, Candy, on his way round the world to study

11

conditions amongst the spastics . . . '
she went on but Candy was not
listening, she was leaning over the
balcony rail, gazing down at the street
below where a *rickshaw boy* was trying
to induce some tourists to get into
his two-wheeled rickshaw, leaping in
the air, his many strings of beads
bouncing, the curved horns on his
head waving precariously as he leapt
in the air, tilting the small rickshaw
backwards.

'It's like being in a different world . . . '
Candy said slowly.

Durban was so beautiful with the
great stretches of golden beaches, the
huge white-capped rollers racing in
from the Indian Ocean, the great luxury
hotels lining the front, the enormous
American cars filling the streets, the
big shops filled with exciting things, the
crowds on the pavements. Everything
about Durban was *big*. Even the crowds
of Africans streaming home from work
at the end of the day, nearly all dressed
in European clothes as they started on

their long bus or train journeys to the townships where they lived — and every now and then, an African girl or man in tribal clothes, with knitting needles stuck in their extraordinary high mud-packed head-dresses, with huge wooden plugs pushed into holes in their ears, with skin skirts and bodices of bright beads. 'It's like being in a different world,' Candy said again.

* * *

Four days later, Candy was waiting in the hall of the hotel. She had already said good-bye to her mother. She stood behind a pillar, a little apart from the holiday-making crowds, nervous now the moment had come. Would she be travelling with Dr. Faulkner, or had he returned to the school already? What would he be like to work for . . .

Suddenly the pretty receptionist brought a tall dark girl to her and said: 'You *are* Miss White?'

When Candy nodded, the receptionist

left them and Candy stared at the dark-haired girl who was, in turn, staring back at her with a very odd expression on her face.

'But you can't possibly be *our* Miss White,' the girl said slowly. 'The new secretary?'

'I am — ' Candy said, instantly on the defence. Then the girl smiled and Candy relaxed. 'Why — who did you expect?' she asked nervously for she had hoped her green linen suit and the rather sober straw hat would impress the school for, as her mother had said, Candy must not *startle* them too soon.

The dark girl who had a dismayed look on her pretty plump face laughed uneasily. 'It's just that you're so young,' she said in a helpless sort of way and then, when Candy made a little grimace, hastily apologised. 'I know how maddening it is to have things like that said about you,' she added. 'Who interviewed you? Not — surely not — Dr. Faulkner?'

'Yes, he did,' Candy told her. 'He did think at first that I might be too young,' she confessed.

'But you convinced him that you are older than you look?' the girl asked in a rather dry voice. 'Sooner you — or rather, sooner he than me . . . ' she said and laughed uneasily and then smiled, a warm friendly smile. 'Forgive me, I don't want to put you off. I am Nancy Boone, the Assistant Matron. The car is outside. Where is your luggage?'

Candy showed her and Nancy told one of the hotel porters to carry the cases outside and then led the way out into the brilliant sunshine to an enormous black car. The door was instantly opened by a very smart, white-coated African chauffeur and Nancy began to chatter right away in a friendly voice, telling her that she was frightfully — but frightfully — glad that Candy was joining the staff as she was the only young one — really young — there.

Soon they left the town behind and

15

were on a wide two-way road but Candy had little time to look at the beautiful hills and valleys for Nancy was telling her about the school and it was too absorbing to miss.

'We're a friendly community — mostly,' Nancy prattled away. 'We have some nice men teachers but most of them are frightfully old — practically ga-ga — but we have our own Wolf, of course.' She laughed happily. 'Trouble is, he isn't a *real* wolf, just likes to pretend to be one so we all play up . . . '

The miles flashed past as Candy listened and gradually built up a composite picture of the school, with many people who were very nice, and a few who were just the opposite.

'Our biggest bear,' Nancy told her, 'is Constance, of course. I mean Miss Faulkner — or the Duchess, as we call her. Not to her face, of course, though the doctor nearly did, one day.' She laughed happily. 'Not that it would have mattered if he had,' she went on, more quietly, 'For he can do no wrong. Most of us hate Constance but then maybe she can't help being as she is, poor thing. Frustrated and all that. She's single, of course and I can't see any man daring to marry her, or surviving if he did . . . ' She laughed and then looked at Candy worriedly. 'Am I being horribly catty? I'm afraid so. I mustn't prejudice you against Constance. She can be quite charming when it suits her but she squeezes the last ounce of work out of everyone. Her last secretary had a nervous breakdown but of course that was largely due to Andrew . . . '

She stopped speaking abruptly, her pretty peach-like skin suddenly flushed, as she pointed to the side of the road. 'Look — a typically African scene,' she said.

Obediently Candy looked, wondering why Nancy was so obviously changing the subject. She saw two small African children, clad in G-strings, herding some thin black and white cattle that were grazing. The small children waved and Nancy waved back.

'We call them *umfaans* . . . — ' Nancy explained. 'The very small children are called *piccannis* — *not* piccaninnies, that's the American word.'

There was a sudden silence and Candy was glad of a chance to look at the rolling mountains and the sweeping green slopes as she gazed out of the window — at the groups of mud and wattle huts, standing in neatly-swept groups — *kraals* they were called, Nancy told her. Outside the huts the African women stood and stared at the passing car, some leaning on the hoes with which they were clearing the ground, many with babies strapped to their backs by thick blankets. Small children, nearly all naked, came running to wave to the car, their little fat tummies distended, the whites of their eyes and teeth showing up in the dark little faces.

They had left the main tarmac road now and were followed by a great cloud of dust as they roared along the earth road. Crossing a bridge over a narrow shallow river, she leaned forward to watch three African girls bending with straight knees to wash their clothes against the rocks in the water. Then she saw a line of donkeys walking slowly — oh so slowly — along the grass by the road's edge, and on one sat a woman, huddled up unhappily as if very sick and it was as if time stood still. It was on a donkey that Mary had ridden into Bethlehem . . .

'What did you think of Dr. Faulkner?' Nancy asked abruptly.

Startled, Candy turned and blinked for a moment, coming back from her thoughts. 'I . . . I thought he was rather nice,' she said slowly. 'A bit young for a headmaster, surely?'

'I suppose he is . . . ' Nancy said in a surprised voice.

'Look — ' Candy cried, forgetting their conversation in her delight as a herd of goats came leaping and scrambling down the side of the mountain, causing the car to slow up. 'Oh look — ' Candy cried again as she pointed to a very small baby goat, keeping very close to his mother. The goats turned their strange pointed faces, their eyes indifferent, their black and white silky coats shining.

It was a long pleasant journey and at one stage Nancy spoke about the children at the school. Candy had begun to have a very odd feeling that this was a school without children for neither Dr. Faulkner, nor Nancy until then, had said much about them.

'We have a few problem children,' Nancy said. 'Mostly those whose parents are divorced or trying to avoid it. I reckon our biggest problem is the Duchess . . . ' She laughed gaily. 'She is what we call a *bulldozer*. She wants everything *her* way and if you don't fall into line, it's just too bad, for *you*!' Nancy said and chuckled but she didn't sound very amused.

Rather nervously Candy began to wonder if she was going to like Miss

Faulkner. Fortunately at that moment they saw a cluster of houses in a distant valley and Nancy told her that it was Nsingisi and then only thirty-five miles to the school. 'It's just a dorp but it is our nearest shopping-centre . . . '

The little town approached as they went down the steep winding hill-road and then they reached it and drove along the single street which was lined with buildings, all covered thickly with dust. There was a donkey and a cart . . . then a wagon with six oxen yoked . . . There were two big cars outside the only hotel. Several stores but they went too fast for her to see much in the windows.

'There's the Court House . . . ' Nancy said, pointing to a straggling sort of tin-roofed building. 'Every Saturday night, we have bioscope there . . . '

Outside the tiny town, Nancy pointed out a thatched-roof house built on a koppie. 'That's South African for a small hill,' Nancy explained patiently. 'That's where the doctor lives. He's

most attractive and great fun but
. . . well, a bit odd. No one knows
why a man so young and so brilliant
and with a good future prefers to bury
himself in a dorp like this. He lives with
his mother and she is a bit queer . . . No
one ever sees her, they never entertain
and she never goes out and the natives
are scared stiff of her, some say she is a
white witch doctor . . . ' Nancy's laugh
rang out.

Now the scenery changed and Candy
looked about with interest as they drove
along a deep cool dark ravine that ran
between towering mountains and then
began to climb again . . . once more
they were high up on a wind-swept
plateau, the valley far below and behind
them.

'There's something that's hard to
credit — ' Nancy said, pointing
to a great white house they were
passing. As they rushed by, Candy
saw a swimming-pool, tennis courts,
a great garden blazing with flowers,
a huge lawn with tables with striped

umbrellas, a wide terrace to the house. 'Sam Covington lives there,' Nancy told her. 'He's a very eccentric millionaire and one of the school directors. He has a daughter but she is at some finishing school in Switzerland.'

Now the car was swooping down into a valley again — but then by the side of a crystal-clear waterfall, the road straightened again and suddenly Nancy cried excitedly — almost proudly: 'There's the school . . . '

2

The Friendly Young Man

Candy gazed up at the huge building and thought it far more beautiful than in the photograph she had seen of it. The great oaken door opened and an African girl stood there in a red dress with a crisply starched apron and a minute white cap perched on top of her dark hair.

Nancy spoke briefly to her and led the way into the lofty raftered hall and up the wide curving staircase. 'I'll take you to your room first,' she said over her shoulder.

Candy's room was small but very pleasant. Palest blue walls with rose-patterned chintz for curtains and matching divan cover. She walked straight to the window, catching her breath with sheer delight as she gazed at peak after peak of mountains, stretching away into the distance.

'I'll give you half-an-hour to wash and brush up and then I'll introduce you to Mrs. Combie,' Nancy said. 'And we'll have some tea before you have to meet Miss Faulkner.' With a friendly grimace, she closed the door.

Alone, Candy hastily unpacked, then washed carefully and brushed her hair vigorously — it was horribly thick with dust — and wished she could let it cluster in wild dark curls, for sweeping it up into a chignon was an awful fag but maybe she had better wear it this severe way for a while longer. Judging from Nancy's comments, Miss Faulkner was due for a nasty shock when she discovers how young her new secretary was! But Dr. Faulkner had engaged her so what could his sister do about it?

It was a relief to get away from worried thoughts when Nancy came to fetch her and led her to Mrs. Combie's private sitting-room. Mrs. Combie, a plump woman with grey hair strained back very severely and wary eyes that betrayed surprise as Nancy introduced Candy.

Nancy burst out laughing. 'She does look young, doesn't she, Mrs. Combie? I told you but you wouldn't believe me, would you? I can't think what Andrew was thinking of . . .'

Candy's smile felt as if it was nailed to her face. Then Mrs. Combie frowned meaningly at Nancy and turned to smile at Candy. 'Welcome, Miss White. I certainly do hope you will be very happy here . . . ' and then she paused and as if the words were wrung out of her, as if she could not resist temptation, she added: 'Dr. Faulkner *did* interview you?'

They were settled in comfortable arm-chairs and Nancy was passing Candy some chicken sandwiches. It was an effort to smile but Candy managed.

'Yes,' she said and added. 'You know, I am not so very young. I am twenty-one. I've worked for nearly two years as secretary to a professor at London University and . . . ' Despite her efforts to hide it, she could hear her defiance and anger in her voice so she made herself smile again. 'Nancy seems to think Miss Faulkner will feel I'm far too young.'

'I'm quite sure she will,' Mrs. Combie said a little grimly. 'But what is done is done. I'm sure I don't understand why . . . ' She paused and smiled at Candy. 'There, childie,' she said in a kind voice. 'It's really too bad of us for scaring you like this. Miss Faulkner can be real nice when she likes and I'm sure if you work hard and do your best to please her, you'll have no cause for complaint — ' Forthwith she changed the subject and asked Candy where she came from, about her parents but all in a very friendly way and in no wise resembling a cross-examination.

As Candy answered the questions she glanced round the pretty, comfortable room and thought that at least, the

Faulkners treated their staff well. She looked out of the window at the wonderful view of the mountains, changing colour now as the sun began to drop. There was a welcome breeze and even the heat was very different from the moist humid heat of Durban.

When they had finished tea, Mrs. Combie took Candy downstairs to the hall and opened a door. 'This will be your office,' she said in a kind voice.

Candy looked round quickly and was glad to see it was a well-equipped room. Fortunately, too, she was familiar with the kind of typewriter, there were good steel filing cabinets, a proper adjustable chair, a big desk with plenty of drawers. The window, though small, gave a wonderful view of the garden and the drive to the front door so she would always be able to see in advance when visitors were arriving.

Mrs. Combie led the way to an inner door and knocked, standing back as she looked down at the nervous face

28

of the slight girl who kept pushing her glasses back on her nose, and smiled reassuringly. 'You'll do . . . ' she whispered. 'I can always *tell*,' she added with a quick encouraging pat on Candy's shoulder, left her.

When a deep voice told her to enter, Candy obeyed, hoping her nervousness didn't show on her face, that her hair would stay up and . . .

It seemed an enormous room and filled with bright sunshine — enormous arched windows with long impressive-looking cream and gold brocade curtains — a thick deep wine-red carpet — great bowls of blue flowers . . . all a vague impression and then she saw thankfully that a tall man was coming to meet her. A man she knew.

'Welcome to Mountain View School, Miss White,' Dr. Faulkner said, taking her hand in his. He was even more handsome than she had remembered and his dark eyes glowed warmly as he smiled down at her. 'I do hope you had a pleasant journey. Have you had some tea? Did Mrs. Combie look after you?' he asked in that deep vibrant voice she had admired before.

All her fears vanished. She was quite unaware that she was still clinging to his hand as if to an anchor until she saw the twinkle in his eyes and then she hastily let go of it and smiled at him; all would be well, he would look after her.

'Oh yes, thank you, it was really a lovely journey and Mrs. Combie gave me a most beautiful tea . . . ' she said eagerly, her words rushing out.

A little cough distracted her attention and she saw a woman sitting behind a small elegant desk. Dr. Faulkner turned and led Candy towards her.

'This is Miss White, Constance,' he said gravely, his smile vanishing.

Candy stared with a sinking heart into a pair of cold dark eyes; shrewd, thoughtful, disapproving eyes. Miss Faulkner was completely unlike her brother. She had none of his good looks, his warmth and friendly charm.

She sat, very upright, her richly-dark brown hair was coiled in neat plaits round her head, her face was beautifully made-up, her grey dress with the simple flashing diamond brooch was elegant but . . .

Involuntarily Candy shivered. Dr. Faulkner spoke again, this time his voice significant as he said: 'You will remember that I told you that Miss White is the daughter of Dr. Elisa White, the famous child specialist.'

'I remember,' his sister said coldly. Then she smiled at Candy — a polite smile. 'Welcome to Mountain View, Miss White. Please sit down for I wish to talk to you. I would prefer us to be alone, Andrew — ' she said coldly to her brother.

Candy wondered at the strange expression on his face as he stared at his sister; she saw the little hesitation he failed to hide and then forgot it as he smiled at her brilliantly. 'But of course, my dear Constance.' He spoke as if amused by her but there was no amusement in his eyes as he looked at his sister. 'Don't forget that Miss White is also my secretary, Constance. I can't allow you to monopolise her. I, too, have a pile of letters waiting for her attention.'

'In good time,' Constance Faulkner said coldly and waited until her brother had left the room then turned to look at Candy. 'Are you really twenty-one?' she asked bluntly.

Candy blushed as she jerked the glasses back up on to the bridge of her nose. Her hands were hot and sticky, her mouth suddenly dry. 'Yes, I am, Miss Faulkner,' she said very politely. 'And I have had nearly two years' experience with . . . '

Miss Faulkner made an imperative movement with her right hand. 'I am aware of that,' she said a little curtly. 'Now there are several things that you must understand about our life here. In the first place, you will work for my brother and myself and will have little to do with the children, and even less with the staff during working hours. Naturally you must remain on friendly terms with them but in view of your extreme youth, I must warn you that we do not tolerate any kind of romantic liasion between members of the staff. You will be required to behave with dignity and discretion and if you do not conduct yourself in such a manner, we shall have to ask you to leave. Have I made myself clear?'

Candy's cheeks were flaming but she swallowed her indignation and merely said very quietly: 'Quite clear. I understand perfectly.'

'Good. We shall get on well so long as we understand one another,' Miss Faulkner said, her voice softening a little. 'Are you tired?' she asked abruptly.

Startled, Candy shook her head. 'Not very. It was a pleasant journey and — '

'Then I wonder if you would type some letters for me right away? They are very urgent for in a few weeks time the term starts. I am very behind as a result of my last secretary's regrettable behaviour . . . ' Miss Faulkner's voice was tart as she rose, two angry flags of colour in her pale cheeks, and sailed — no other word for it, Candy thought as she followed — into the office and gave her a wire basket piled with letters, to each of which was attached a note. She showed Candy where the stationery was kept and said abruptly: 'Leave the letters on my desk when you have finished them and I will sign them. In the morning I will tell you what your duties will be. Mrs. Combie will look after you this evening.' She turned and left Candy.

Alone, Candy saw with relief that the notes were all written in a beautiful copper-plate handwriting and very easy to read. She took out paper, carbons and envelopes and got down to work and soon felt at ease, getting through the letters at a satisfactory speed. How much easier when you could read the words at the first glance and didn't have to peer and guess and compare as she had always had to do when reading the professor's scribbled notes!

She gave a little start of surprise when suddenly the door to the hall burst open and a man walked into the room. Hands pausing on the keys, Candy stared at him. He stared back.

He was a young man, tall, too thin, with blond hair cut very short and hazel eyes which were very startled as he looked at her. He wore khaki shorts and a jacket and he carried an incongruous-looking black bag in his hand.

He pointed a long finger at her and said in a hushed voice: 'Oh no . . . ' He gave a little moan but she saw that his eyes were dancing with amusement. 'Don't tell me that Andrew has gone quite mad and that you are the new secretary?' He whistled very softly. 'Or has Connie gone off her head?'

Candy's face stiffened with anger as she said coldly: 'I am the new secretary and I was engaged by Dr. Faulkner . . . ' She was thoroughly tired of the incessant idiotic jokes about her youth! 'And I am twenty-one,' she added firmly.

The young man stared at her and his face seemed to crinkle with laughter. But though it was hilarious it was also silent laughter. He kept shaking his head and trying to look serious but in the end, he plonked his bag on the ground and perched on the edge of her desk, staring down at her angry startled face until he got his voice back. 'I apologise . . . ' he said in a trembling voice. 'Humbly and with intent to make amends.' His eyes were still twinkling. 'You are twenty-one, experienced in clerical work and old enough to know what you are doing. I get it — and I won't forget it.' He grinned at her. It was a rather attractive lop-sided sort of smile. 'Honestly I am sorry' . . . he said, more gravely and she saw that he meant it. 'It's just that . . . Have you seen the Duchess yet?' he asked, lowering his voice.

'If you are referring to Miss

Faulkner . . . ' Candy began stiffly.

'Who else?' the young man asked. Then his voice became sober and a little anxious. 'When did you arrive?'

Startled, Candy blurted out. 'This . . . this afternoon.'

He frowned at her. 'And she's got you working already? Typical, of course. You must be whacked to the wide.'

The sympathy in his voice thawed the resentment that still lingered despite his apology. 'I didn't think I was tired . . . ' she admitted slowly. 'But I am . . . ' She pushed her glasses back up her nose and sighed.

'Look,' he advised, 'Pack up. She's not a bad old bird at heart. She'd be most upset if she knew you were tired and battling. Tomorrow is another day . . . '

She half-smiled and then glanced down at the pile of letters she had typed. 'I've nearly finished and . . . '

'First impressions are so important, eh?' he finished for her quietly and with a friendly smile. 'You know,

37

you'd be much more comfortable if those spectacles of yours fitted properly. They keep slipping.' Before she could stop him, he leaned towards her and took off the glasses, holding them up to the light. He whistled softly and gave them back to her. 'Camouflage?' he asked.

She slipped them on quickly, giving them an impatient little jerk into place. 'I wanted the job badly . . . ' she said simply.

He gave her a warm smile. 'I'll keep your secret,' he promised, and somehow she knew he was a man who kept his word. He looked towards the inner door. 'Is she in?'

'I'll see,' Candy said and went to the door. 'What name shall I say?' she asked, turning to smile at him.

'Bill . . . ' He stood up and shrugged. 'No, better say Dr. Abbott,' he told her. 'First impressions, you know,' he added, smiling down at her, 'I wouldn't want her to think we were on first name terms already . . . ' His eyes were twinkling as he came towards her. 'But I hope we are. What's your name?'

'Candace . . . ' she told him and knocked on the door.

She heard Miss Faulkner answer before the doctor had time to say anything so she opened the door quickly and Miss Faulkner looked up from her desk coldly.

'What is it?' There was an impatient note in her voice.

'Dr. Abbott,' Candy began but the young doctor walked past her and Candy saw Miss Faulkner's face come to life: became warm, welcoming, almost beautiful.

As she closed the door, Candy heard the doctor say: 'I hate to have to tell you, Constance, but . . . '

Back at her desk, Candy stared out of the window thoughtfully. So that was the odd doctor Nancy had told her about . . . the doctor who was buried here in the *bundu* for some mysterious reason, whose mother frightened the Africans.

As she began to type again, she decided to take everything Nancy said with a big grain of salt. There was nothing 'odd' about that friendly young doctor . . . She began to hum under her breath. It looked as if this job was going to be fun, after all.

3

A Battle of Wits

Candy had just finished the last of the letters when the inner door suddenly opened and Bill Abbott came through. He looked at her quickly and she wondered why he looked so bleak and unhappy but he gave her a quick smile as he rushed by.

'Be seeing you . . . got to hurry . . . ' he said.

It was like a whirlwind dashing through the office and she wondered why she got the impression that he was in a furious temper. She took the letters to the inner room but Miss Faulkner had gone — doubtless through the other door though Candy did not know where it led to . . . Glad of the respite for she had had enough of Miss Faulkner for one day, Candy left the letters on the desk.

On her way upstairs, she met Nancy.

'So she didn't eat you?' Nancy teased.

'She merely nibbled . . . ' Candy said and found she could laugh at the joke herself.

In a way, it was funny. At least if a friendly nice man like Bill Abbott saw it as a joke, then it must be one. Perhaps Miss Faulkner had a 'thing' about young people, and of course the little lecture about behaviour was obviously a stock lecture and used for everyone.

At dinner — an ample, well-cooked meal which they ate in the staff room, Candy met the Matron, a thin, grey-haired woman with a mouth like a nutcracker but, according to Nancy who was not given to praising people, a heart of gold. She, at least, did not comment on Candy's youth but merely remarked that she looked tired and that to someone unaccustomed to it, the altitude could be very tiring, and an early night might be a good idea. Candy heartily agreed and was glad to have a hot bath and crawl into bed.

She had been told her day's work would start at eight o'clock *sharp* so she was waiting in her office at ten minutes to the hour, trying not to feel nervous, constantly pushing her glasses back up on her nose, hoping her demure white and blue cotton frock would be dignified enough to please Miss Faulkner.

At exactly eight o'clock Miss Faulkner walked into the office and found Candy cleaning her typewriter.

She looked surprised. 'Good morning. I trust you will continue to be as punctual,' she said dryly.

Candy had planned a campaign of action. She was going to be the perfect secretary for she was determined to stay out her six months, so she was not going to give Miss Faulkner a chance to find fault with her. Not if she could help it.

'My mother says punctuality is one

of the greatest virtues,' Candy said now a little primly.

Miss Faulkner looked at her sharply but there was no mirth on Candy's face, not even in her eyes.

'Your mother is quite right,' Miss Faulkner said a little grimly. 'I also note that you can spell correctly and know something about punctuation. Thank you for getting through all the letters. I did not expect them all done.'

'They were so easy to do, Miss Faulkner,' Candy said earnestly — and truthfully. 'Your writing is so beautiful and easy to read.'

Miss Faulkner frowned. 'I prefer to dictate . . . '

Candy nodded. 'Of course. I understand that in the circumstances . . . '

'I wonder if you do,' Miss Faulkner said strangely and instantly began to show Candy the post book and where the stamps were kept; she told her that she had to keep the correspondence of Dr. Faulkner as well as her own up to

44

date, take down telephone messages. 'Intelligently. Always make sure you have the name correctly. Now I've some letters to dictate. When they are typed, enter them in the book and stamp them. Be careful about that, too, for the air mail letters are entered in a separate book . . . '

Candy took her notebook and pencils — fortunately she had sharpened four in readiness — and sat demurely in a chair to take dictation.

Bent over her notebook, it was hard to hide her amusement for Miss Faulkner dictated at a terrific rate, so fast that at first Candy wondered if she could read her outlines back for it had been some time since she did any shorthand, and then, suddenly, Miss Faulkner seemed to weary of the effort to trip Candy up and her dictation grew slower and slower. Inside her, Candy was chuckling away madly. So it was to be a fight, was it? Miss Faulkner wanted to defeat her, to be able to accuse her of inefficiency? Candy's mouth tightened and her small stubborn chin lifted. If that was the way Miss Faulkner wanted to play it, Candy was game. It made the job more interesting to realise it was going to be a battle of wits.

'That will be all — for now,' Miss Faulkner said curtly. 'I'd like these typed right away.' Even as she spoke the second door opened and her brother came in. He greeted Candy politely, barely looking at her, frowning as he saw the letters she was gathering up.

'Constance,' he said and he sounded vexed. 'You told me Miss White had got your correspondence up to date. Now why must you dictate more letters when you know I have a pile waiting . . . '

'My dear Andrew,' Miss Faulkner said smoothly. 'I waited until a quarter past eight but as you did not come through, I thought you must have other plans. Miss White shouldn't be long doing these and then she can attend to you.' She turned to Candy. 'Do you know your way to my brother's study?'

Candy stared at her. 'No, Miss Faulkner. I hardly know my way around yet. Only the staff dining-room and . . . '

'Of course,' Miss Faulkner snapped. Candy made a mental note that Miss Faulkner liked short, to-the-point answers. 'When you have finished these and I have signed them and you have stamped and entered *all* the letters, ring the bell and Petrus will take you to my brother's study. Those few shouldn't take you long . . . ' she finished, turned her back on Candy and began to speak to her brother quietly.

A little vexed, Candy retreated to her own office. Miss Faulkner certainly squeezed the last ounce of work out of her secretary. It was a fearsome pile of work, then the entries and the stamps . . .

Biting her lip, she began to type rapidly. Fortunately she found it easy enough to read back what she had written down. Her wretched glasses kept slipping, and she felt like cursing the day she bought them for they were nothing but a nuisance, but at least, they did make her look a little older. None of the letters was very long, mostly to parents and enclosing a prospectus, many to other parents saying regretfully that at the moment there were no vacancies. It seemed hours before she had finished them all, had them signed, then stamped and entered them and it was with a sigh that she rang the bell and Petrus, a tall thin African with a high cheek-boned face and soft husky voice, led her down the hall and along a corridor that obviously passed behind Miss Faulkner's room and finally led her to Dr. Faulkner's study.

Dr. Faulkner looked surprised to see her. Leapt to his feet and brought forward a chair. It was a big room, as big as his sister's but completely different. Not only was it a very masculine room but it was far more comfortable. The desk was enormous and her chair just the right shape and the light did not seem so glaring for the walls were panelled and there were heavy curtains, and the only flowers were a pot of flowering red fuschias.

'I didn't expect you for hours yet, Miss White,' he said frankly. 'I thought my sister had given you a pile of work.'

Candy felt herself relax. In here, she was with a friend. 'It was rather a lot,' she confessed, 'but luckily I type fast.'

He became very business-like and her pencil flew over the pages. In the middle of a letter the point cracked and she apologised and even as she took a second pencil out of her pocket, he was leaning forward to offer her one.

He smiled. 'Bright girl,' he said approvingly. 'You're the first secretary we've had who was prepared for any emergency.'

Candy smiled back. 'We were trained to be.'

He dictated faster than Constance but well. He would read the letter through, think for a moment, then walk about the room, hands clasped behind him, head slightly bent, eyes narrowed as he dictated, hardly looking at her. She was thankful when at last he finished for her hand was quite cramped. The letters dated back a very long way, much further back than Miss Faulkner's letters. How was it he was so behind-hand? No wonder he had been vexed with his sister.

He towered above her as she collected the letters. 'Tomorrow will do for these,' he said curtly. 'No hurry.'

She opened her mouth and closed it again, taking the letters to her office and starting to type them, continuing after lunch, even though Nancy told her that as a rule, the secretary didn't have to type in the afternoon.

'I'd sooner get them done,' Candy said doggedly. She had a horrible feeling that she must keep up-to-date or Miss Faulkner would swoop and pounce on her like a relentless eagle and produce more work.

Nancy brought her a cup of tea

and shook her head. 'Don't be a clot, Candy,' she said softly. 'Connie will only pile stuff on you.'

Candy smiled back, her voice also low. 'She will in any case. I don't want to be caught napping.'

There was sudden understanding in Nancy's eyes. 'You're doing battle?' she whispered and when Candy nodded, Nancy chuckled. 'Good luck. You'll need it.'

When the very last letter and envelope had been typed and put neatly in a wire basket, Candy sighed with relief and pulled her cover over the typewriter. She hurried along the corridor and the polished floor tempted her and the next moment, she was sliding gaily along.

A tall thin figure walked out of a doorway and Candy slithered to a standstill just in time! As near as anything, she had bumped into Miss Faulkner who stood staring at her, silent for a moment and shocked.

'Really, Miss White,' Miss Faulkner said acidly. 'You must remember that you are no longer a school-girl. Kindly comport yourself with dignity.'

'I'm sorry,' Candy said and meant it, she had forgotten her 'position' for a moment but that was no excuse. 'I was in a hurry.'

'That may be but it is no excuse for you to behave like a young hooligan.' Miss Faulkner said coldly. 'Kindly see that it does not occur again.'

'Yes, Miss Faulkner . . . I mean, no . . . ' Candy began, a little confused but Miss Faulkner was no longer listening, sailing down the corridor, with dignity comporting herself, Candy thought, with a hastily suppressed giggle.

Dr. Faulkner looked startled when she gave him the letters. 'My dear girl,' he said in a slightly annoyed voice. 'We are not slave drivers. There was no need to do them . . . '

She waited while he signed them. Her head ached and her back was stiff.

'I know, sir,' she said very politely.

'But if I had left them to the morning, Miss Faulkner might have required my services.'

He looked up at her quickly, as if startled by some note in her voice. 'Well, thank you . . . anyway . . . They are very well done . . . ' he said.

She took the tray. 'Thank you, sir.'

She had her hand on the door knob when he called: 'Miss White . . . ' As she turned to look at him, he asked: 'Can you drive?'

A little startled, she told him that she could. 'Mother has a car and I have my driving licence.'

'Good — ' he said, smiling at her. 'I'll arrange for you to have a test out here for we may be glad to have you use the car. Often the chauffeur is engaged and you may be asked to go into Nsingisi for the mail or with a child. You would not mind?'

For a moment, she thought of the steep mountainous roads, the sharp bends, the sudden drops, the dark ravine, and then she smiled at him.

'I should enjoy it,' she said.

'Good.' He smiled at her. 'Good.'

She went in search of Nancy and found her sprawled on her bed, reading a magazine, her hair in curlers. Nancy sat up: 'You look very pleased with yourself — you ought to be dead tired,' she said.

Candy collapsed into Nancy's chair. 'I am — actually,' she confessed. 'Dr. Faulkner wants me to drive the car . . .' she said and smiled.

Nancy reacted satisfactorily and whistled. 'Well, I'm . . . You are honoured. That's more than he ever let Cartwright do and he . . .' She paused and stared at Candy, amusement in her eyes. 'How do you do it, honey? You've got him eating out of your hand and even got the Duchess taped . . .'

'Don't reckon on that,' Candy said dryly. 'I'm sure she has plenty of tricks up her sleeve . . .' She accepted a cigarette and relaxed in the chair, glad the working day was finished. 'I wonder why she hates me so . . . why she wants to make me fed-up with the job . . . '

Nancy hugged her knees and rocked herself. 'Actually I don't think she hates you, Candy, nor does she want to get rid of you. It's the way she's made. She automatically works everyone to death.'

Candy blew several smoke rings thoughtfully. 'Then it's not me?'

Nancy began to laugh, deftly pulling out the curlers. 'Heavens no, Candy. She gave Cartwright a bad time, especially after . . . ' She paused. 'Maybe that was different . . . ' she said thoughtfully. 'Be a lamb and comb out my hair for me, Candy?'

'Of course . . . ' Candy said and stood up at once, smiling at Nancy and wondering what life would be like here without her. It made everything so much easier when you had a friend with whom you could discuss things.

At dinner that night, Nancy introduced Candy to a short, dark, handsome man who limped towards them, his eyes bright with admiration.

'This is our wolf . . . ' Nancy said gaily. 'Bob Robinson. He is supposed to teach art, but all he does is break 'earts . . . ' she rocked with laughter.

Bob Robinson's face turned a dull red. 'Oh, shut up, Nancy,' he said but his voice was good-tempered. 'I've just had a lecture from the Duchess herself but how do I stop a teenager from falling for me? They mean no harm. They're bound to weave dreams at that age and I happened to be handy. What am I to do?' He smiled at Candy. 'Let me guess — you're our new dancing teacher.'

'Wrong — ' Nancy shrieked, rocking with laughter. 'She's the new secretary.'

'You don't say . . . ' Bob said in an awed voice. He pretended to collapse in a chair, shaded his eyes and peered at Candy. 'How on earth did you sneak past the the portals?'

'I was . . . ' Candy began stiffly, her liking for him vanishing.

'Let me . . . ' Nancy said quickly. She put her finger on her chin and looked very meek. 'I am twenty-one, have had two years' experience and was interviewed by Dr. Faulkner in Durban — ' she said, mimicking Candy's voice perfectly.

'Nancy girl, go and get me a cold drink. I'm dying of thirst after all that dust . . . ' Bob said quickly and when Nancy smiled at him and obediently trotted off, he turned to Candy, taking in every detail of the angry pretty little face that looked so small behind the enormous spectacles that she kept jerking into place. 'Nancy's humour is somewhat heavy at times,' he said gently. 'You mustn't let it get you down.'

She smiled at him gratefully. 'I try not to but . . . but I can never see the joke . . . '

At that moment a tall, well-built woman with beautifully waved, smoky-grey hair came into the room. Bob was on his feet instantly.

'Philippa . . . my dear Philippa . . . ' he said, his voice warm and sincere.

57

'Are you really well enough to come back?'

The middle-aged woman smiled at him. 'Quite well, thank you, Bob.' She looked at Candy and smiled. 'You are Miss White? I am Miss Rowland,' she said, holding out her hand in greeting.

'The Duchess' right hand,' Bob said, pushing a chair forward for the newcomer. 'What should we all do without you? Now, Philippa.' He hitched his chair forward, his face alight with mischief. 'Don't you think it rather strange that this nice little bit of sweetness should be the secretary?'

Miss Rowland smiled at Candy. 'I do see what you mean, Bob, but I understand that we are very fortunate to have her. I am told she is the most efficient secretary we have ever had, that she can spell, type without error and is very quick.'

Candy glowed with delight at the praise. 'Whoever said that?'

Miss Rowland smiled at her. 'Miss Faulkner herself, and believe me, that is high praise from her.'

'I know it is,' Candy said fervently, suddenly feeling very happy. It was the sort of remark she could have expected from Dr. Faulkner but it was much more satisfying to have his sister say it. She happened to turn her head at that moment and wondered vaguely why Bob was smiling but then Miss Rowland was asking her how much of the school she had seen.

'We mustn't overwork you, Miss White,' she said in her gentle voice. 'Miss Faulkner does not always realise the extent of her demands. What is your Christian name?'

Candy smiled at her. 'Candace — ' she said and waited for laughter.

'A very pretty name — ' Miss Rowland began but Nancy returned at that moment with a glass of tomato juice for Bob.

She fell on Miss Rowland excitedly. 'How lovely to see you — we were so afraid you wouldn't be back this term.' She smiled at Candy. 'Isn't it lovely for me to have someone of my own age? Her name is Candace but I call her Candy.'

'Candy — ' Bob said, a strange smile on his long thin face. 'It suits you. Sugar and spice and all that's nice . . . '

Candy laughed and wondered why Nancy gave her a quick startled look and then Miss Rowland was saying: 'Candace is a little long and rather old for you, my dear. So we'll call you Candy out of working hours, if that is all right?'

Candy smiled. She liked Miss Rowland; she liked Bob Robinson, and Nancy was her friend. This job was definitely going to be fun, and not only a battle of wits with Miss Faulkner. 'I'd feel happier,' she said. 'When someone says *Miss White*, I'm apt to look over my shoulder to see who they're talking to . . . '

Everyone laughed and Candy smiled at them all. How glad she was she had applied for this job!

4

Her Opinion is Sought

Miss Rowland's arrival seemed to have touched a switch that set everything in motion for suddenly things began to happen. The staff began to arrive and Candy found herself doing all sorts of strange jobs and always, deftly, Miss Rowland seemed to intervene between Candy and Miss Faulkner's most excessive demands, and as a result, Candy really enjoyed her life. It was no longer merely clerical work. Miss Rowland taught her to show parents round the school; how to entertain them while they waited to see one of the principals. Candy found herself acquiring an almost personal pride in the school. She thought it a wonderful place and said so in one of her frequent letters to her mother.

'I'm so happy here, Mummy,' she wrote. 'And everything is lovely. It is a truly wonderful school.'

She was a little shaken with her mother's reply but afterwards saw the wisdom and justice of her words.

'I am very glad you are so happy, darling, but I'll be more interested to hear what you think of the school once term starts. It is easy enough to have a model school when there are no children in it. Once the children are there — that is the true test of a good school.'

Almost every day a fresh member of the staff turned up; a few of them were, but all, of course, were new to Candy. There was Greta Stromberg, the massive blonde with huge biceps who taught German; a pretty dark-haired woman with large provocative eyes and very elegant clothes who taught French — these two largely ignored both Candy and Nancy. Then there was Horace Hyde who taught history and English and was middle-aged with a small moustache and a kindly tact that kept the staff-room harmonious, and Malcolm Fenn, the Science Master, frail and with an ugly plainness that had a charm of its own, who spent most of his time hidden behind a newspaper but always thawed for Candy and would spend hours talking about London to her.

One morning, Candy went up to Sick Bay to ask the Matron about some drugs that had to be ordered and, as she pushed the heavy swing door open, she recognised Dr. Abbott's voice and felt absurdly pleased because, although she had seen him several times in the distance, they had not spoken. He was talking to Matron and they did not stop when Candy entered. Later she wondered if they had even seen her.

'I tried but I failed — ' Bill Abbott was saying.

'If anyone could persuade her, you're

the one, Bill,' Matron told him comfortingly.

He shrugged. 'It's not as simple as that, believe me. This other business. I can't understand how he could do such a thing, especially so soon. I mean there was trouble enough last time . . . '

Matron sounded amused. 'My dear, don't you know there's no fool like an old fool, unless it be a young one.'

'Sometimes I think I'm developing an allergy like Bob's . . . ' he said almost sheepishly and then he saw Candy and his face brightened. 'Hi — ' he said cheerfully. 'You're still with us.'

Candy smiled at him as she walked her short brisk little steps.

'And determined to remain . . . ' she said happily.

She had not realised he was so good-looking or maybe it was the dark suit, the good dark blue silk tie, the highly polished shoes — or could it have been because his very blond hair had been severely brushed? 'I'm glad you like it here,' he said gravely and she saw that he meant it. Then he turned to the woman by her side in her starched uniform and smiled into her wise eyes, his voice suddenly gay. 'Well, Matron mine, I'm off for a few days but I'll be back in time for school to start.' He smiled at Candy. 'We usually start term with a few ailments, don't we, Matron, but we just take it in our stride. I'm off to Durban and have an important appointment with a gentleman . . . yes, Matron,' he said smiling at the tall woman who shook her head disbelievingly. 'A gentleman — cross my heart . . . '

'You're sure it isn't with a pretty lady, Bill?' Matron's face clouded as she looked at him anxiously. 'You're not thinking of leaving us, lad?'

He laughed at that. 'Not likely. You won't get rid of me so easily.'

Matron did not smile. 'We don't want to, Bill. You're essential to our well-being.' Her face changed again and she spoke almost cautiously: 'Are you taking your mother with you?'

His face clouded. 'How can I? She won't budge,' he said with a strange bitterness that disturbed Candy. Then he was smiling again. 'Well — good-bye, both of you. Don't do anything I wouldn't . . . ' he said cheerily just as if that dark bleak moment had never existed, and then he was walking with long swift strides down the ward and through the swing door.

There was an odd little silence and then Matron spoke slowly. 'Now, there's a good lad. A good lad and don't let anyone tell you differently, my dear.'

A little startled by her gravity, Candy said: 'I hardly know him but he is always friendly.'

'Aye, he's a good lad,' the Matron repeated. 'Now — what can I do for you?'

That evening, Candy found herself sitting next to Bob at dinner for there was an unwritten rule that no one had a set place. As they were talking, she remembered the conversation she had overheard in Sick Bay and on an impulse, she turned to Bob and said: 'What are you allergic to, Bob?'

His dark eyes looked startled. 'Who suggested I was allergic to anything?' he asked.

Candy was rather sorry she had brought up the subject and looked round a little nervously but luckily no one was paying them any attention, being engrossed in conversation, so she told Bob the truth. 'I went to Sick Bay to see Matron and I heard Dr. Abbott telling her that he was getting your allergy . . . '

She was quite unprepared for his great shout of laughter and felt horribly conspicuous as the others merely looked down the table and smiled and then carried on their own conversations. She sat very still, cheeks red with embarrassment while Bob coughed and choked himself to soberness. His eyes twinkling as he looked at her, he said quietly: 'The only thing I'm allergic to is women . . . Maybe that is what Bill meant?' His eyes were amused and Candy felt even more confused. Was that what the doctor had meant? As she looked at Bob, she jerked her glasses into place irritably and then her eyes widened in dismay. 'You hate women?' she said.

He patted her hand. 'I don't hate *you*, Candy, quite the reverse, but at the risk of appearing most abominably conceited and in fact, a bit of a cad,' he was smiling at her so she was not sure if he was serious or not as he went on: 'I quite frankly find that women chase me and if there is one thing I do like to do, it is my own hunting.'

'I see,' she said in a very small voice. Had Dr. Abbott meant that some woman was chasing him? Or had he another reason for disliking women? Yet he didn't seem to — he was so friendly . . . 'Would you say, then, that Dr. Abbott is allergic to women?' she asked Bob quietly.

His eyes danced. 'First I've heard of it. Not that he has a girl friend though I believe there are several girls who would like the position, but then Bill is handicapped, you see. His mother . . .' Bob lowered his voice. 'I don't know any facts but they do say she's mad.'

Then it wasn't just Nancy's habit of exaggerating? Candy remembered Bill's bitter voice that morning and how quickly he had conquered it. 'Do you think she is really . . .' Candy said slowly and unhappily.

Bob glanced at her. 'No one knows. No one has ever seen her. They never entertain and she never goes out. The African servants are terrified of her. It's a real tragedy and I think Bill is pretty wonderful the way he hides his feelings.'

'Yes, I think he is,' Candy said thoughtfully.

'Candy — ' Nancy called down the table. 'Who do you think has the biggest teen-age fan-mail? Elvis — Adam Faith — Pat Boone . . .'

Candy turned to smile. 'Oh, I wouldn't know but . . . ' she began and the conversation became general.

The next day, Dr. Faulkner asked her if she had time to take down a few letters. Gladly Candy followed him into his study for she always enjoyed working for him; he never tried to trip her up with long words or by dictating very rapidly, as Miss Faulkner still did at times.

When he had finished his dictation and she was gathering the letters and closing her notebook, he went to sit down opposite her and said abruptly:

'Don't go yet, Miss White, I want to talk to you.'

A little curious, Candy put down her book and sat back, clasping her hands demurely on the lap of her rose-pink shirtwaister. She was slowly *breaking-in* the school to her brightly-coloured clothes and so far, no comment had been made, but Nancy thought it a huge joke for she knew the contents of Candy's wardrobe and knew just how gay Candy could be.

'Miss White — ' Dr. Faulkner began slowly, twirling his tortoise-shell rimmed glasses gently in his hands, his eyes thoughtful as he surveyed her young eager face. 'You have been with us only a short while but often an unbiased fresh pair of eyes can discern points that we, so familiar with the school, might overlook. What is your honest opinion of Mountain View School?'

Candy considered him — and the question — gravely. He really wanted her opinion and was not just asking her a polite question.

'I think it is a wonderful school,' she said slowly. 'I only wish I had been lucky enough to come here. It seems to me that everything a child can want or need is provided here.' She paused, racking her brains for an *intelligent* remark and then remembering her mother's letter. 'Of course, it is impossible to get the *feel* of a school until the term actually starts,' she said, rather pompously, she felt, but he looked quite impressed so she went on. 'If I may say so, Dr. Faulkner, it is easy to have a model school when there are no children present,' she said and was rewarded by the surprise in his eyes. 'The true test comes with the children.'

Dr. Faulkner leaned back in his chair, put on his glasses and stared at her, his dark handsome face thoughtful. 'A very shrewd remark, Miss White. I appreciate your candour. It was wrong of me to ask your opinion at this stage. The building meets with your approval?'

She looked at him quickly because of the strange note in his voice. Was he being sarcastic? Her cheeks felt hot but when he smiled, she saw that he had not taken offence at what she had said but was seriously asking her opinion. She relaxed and smiled back at him. 'I think it is a very beautiful place,' she said in her natural, quick, eager way of speaking. 'Too, too lovely. I think they are very lucky children and if they are only half as happy as I am here . . . '

Dr. Faulkner smiled. 'I am glad you are happy,' he said. He held out a heavy silver cigarette case and smiled at her again. 'You are not being interviewed now, so can't you relax for once? I'm sure your mother would approve,' he added, his eyes twinkling.

Candy took the cigarette and waited while he got up and came with a matching silver lighter to light it for her. She lay back in her chair and felt at ease, looking round her.

'I love this room,' she said.

'So do I . . . ' he said, still smiling at her, his face relaxed. 'It is a good thing for I spend a lot of time in it. Once the term starts, though, I shan't see so much of it.'

'Do you teach?' she asked. It was the first time she had ventured to ask him a question about his life.

'Of course,' he said and looked rather

surprised. 'I teach history, geography, literature . . . '

He was still talking about his method of teaching when she had stubbed out her cigarette. Thinking that maybe she had overstayed her welcome, Candy began to gather her notebook and papers together.

'Thank you for the cigarette — ' she said, as she rose.

He stood up as well and seemed to tower above her so that she had to lean her head back to see him. 'We must do this again,' he told her in his warm friendly voice. 'I feel relaxed. I find it most restful to talk to you.'

She was on her way to the door but now she stopped and turned, her cheeks glowing with pleasure. 'Oh, thank you,' she said and smiled at him, a little shyly now. 'I like talking to you, too.'

He stared at her across the room.

They both stood very still.

'I'm glad you are happy here,' he said in a strange voice.

'I was so afraid I wouldn't prove

satisfactory,' she confessed with an engaging frankness. 'Everyone seemed to think I was too young.'

'I know,' he admitted. 'So did I. But I took a chance and I'm very glad that I did.'

'So am I — ' she said shyly and wondered why she felt so breathless.

Neither moved but both stood silently, staring at one another across the room, and then Candy had to force herself to look away from him, to move to the door, to go outside and leave him . . .

Back in her own office, she sat for a long time just staring at the typewriter. Why had he looked at her like that? What did it mean?

5

The Most Natural Thing

As the beginning of the term drew closer, Candy found herself with more work than ever, for now the different members of the staff brought her their schedules and lists; and there were typed timetables to do as well, often to be altered and re-typed. Everyone was most apologetic and grateful. In addition, Dr. Faulkner took Candy out in the car several times, making her familiar with the different type of gears, finally saying that she was ready for her test as soon as he could arrange for her to take one. It had been rather terrifying to drive on such mountainous roads for everything was so different from driving in England, but Dr. Faulkner had been very patient and had told her finally that she was an excellent pupil. In addition, more and more of the staff were arriving at the school and Candy found it hard to sort out their names for now the staff-room in the evenings seemed full of people, voices, laughter, smoke. Everyone seemed a little on edge; Miss Faulkner was irritable, finding fault where there was none to be found, but Nancy said it was the usual beginning-of-term nerves and they would all soon get over it. Even Nancy had a big moan for with so many new children coming, dormitories had to be reorganised and this involved a lot of work.

'If we go on increasing at this rate,' Nancy said one evening as she sat on Candy's bed and they drank their usual cup of chocolate, 'They'll have to enlarge the school. I think we're big enough. If we get too many pupils, it will spoil the atmosphere but there, what's the good of talking? Miss Faulkner wants the money to come in and new pupils mean more money.'

Two days before the term began,

Dr. Faulkner told Candy that always before the term started, they had a social evening in Nsingisi. 'We dine at the hotel and then dance,' he said. 'It gives the staff a chance to meet the local people and it is a sort of last fling before the hard work commences. Would you like to join us?'

Impulsively Candy clasped her hands. 'I'd love to,' she said eagerly. Nancy had told her of the little regular party but had said rather gloomily that as no one had mentioned it so far, she thought Miss Faulkner had clamped down and cancelled it, for Miss Faulkner did not approve of what she called 'riotous living'. Nancy had laughed rather bitterly and said that she would be interested in Candy's opinion on just how *riotous* living could be when it came to the Nsingisi Hotel!

Now Dr. Faulkner was looking at Candy in distress. 'You have missed your gay life . . . ' he said.

Candy coloured for in a way, it was true. It had been a lot of hard work and no fun up to date. 'Oh no, I haven't,' she said hastily, smiling at him. 'There really hasn't been time and in London, I'm not so very gay although I do go out to dances and Mother and I go to all the shows in town but I'm not really *gay*.'

'You must have lots of boy friends there,' Dr. Faulkner said slowly, his handsome face kind and concerned as he gazed down at her. 'Don't you miss them?'

Candy looked startled. 'No — you see, I haven't got a *special* boy friend. I just like them all. Maybe that makes a difference.'

He was smiling. 'I should imagine it would,' he said dryly. 'Well, I think we shall all benefit from an evening of relaxation, Miss White . . . ' he added curtly and turned away. He had a habit of changing abruptly from being friendly to being almost off-hand. Now he turned and looked at her sternly: 'You worked late again last night? I thought so. I had no idea you were working so late or so often. Next term we must make a different arrangement, get in a temporary typist to help you with some of the extra work. Miss Rowland tells me she is quite worried about it. I can only say I had no idea such a burden of work was being put on your shoulders and apologise . . . ' he spoke jerkily, formally, but she saw that he was sincerely upset.

'Oh please, Dr. Faulkner,' she said earnestly, jerking her glasses back into position, her eyes worried. 'I've loved every moment of it. I knew that the extra work wouldn't be for always and . . . '

Dr. Faulkner smiled. 'Well, if you won't let me apologise, I can at least thank you,' he said and turned to a cupboard behind his desk, taking out a package, giving it to Candy with a shy smile. 'I thought you might enjoy some chocolates . . . '

It was an enormous box with a gorgeous cover of blue silk, decorated by a silk rose. 'Oh, it is lovely,' she said, her eyes shining. 'I'll think of you every time I eat a chocolate,' she promised.

He began to laugh. 'So long as you don't think you are eating me,' he said, 'and develop a cannibalistic appetite.'

Candy began to laugh as well when the door opened and Miss Faulkner appeared: 'What is all the noise about . . . ?' she asked fretfully, her face cold with displeasure.

Dr. Faulkner moved, deftly hiding Candy from his sister. 'That will be all, Miss White,' he said curtly over his shoulder and as he spoke to Miss Faulkner, Candy seized the chance to slip out of the room quickly.

Nancy stared in amazement at the box of chocolates when she saw it. Her eyes were worried as she stared at Candy who was busy opening the box.

'But why did he give it to you?'

Candy was comparing the chocolates with the diagram on the lid.

'Ah . . . ' she said triumphantly,

pouncing on a strawberry-filled choco-late. 'Just a thank-you for all the evenings I've worked late,' she said gaily. 'It has been a bit of a rush, you know, Nancy, and he seemed quite upset about it. Seems Philippa had told him I was grossly overworked . . . ' she chuckled happily. 'I must save some for her, as sort of commission,' she chuckled again. 'Do help yourself, Nancy. There are masses here and I can be quite piggy where chocolates are concerned.'

Nancy carefully chose a hard-centred one. 'Do you like Dr. Faulkner?' she asked casually.

'Oh, very much,' Candy said at once. 'He's marvellous to work for, Nancy. So considerate and appreciative. It does make a difference when people thank you . . . '

'I'll say it does . . . ' Nancy agreed fervently as she took another chocolate. 'These are delicious. Must have cost the earth . . . '

'I think it was sweet of him to

give them to me, don't you, Nancy?' Candy asked her, searching for another strawberry-filled chocolate.

Nancy gave her an odd look. 'Very sweet of him,' she said dryly.

Candy sprang to her feet. 'I'm just going to take some along to Philippa Rowland . . . Be back soon,' she said, flashing a smile at Nancy, who sat for a long time just staring worriedly at the door.

They dressed with great care before the evening's outing. It was odd how important and thrilling just a dinner at a local hotel could be when life had been rather dingy and dull.

'I don't know why we bother,' Nancy grumbled. 'The local people are not very friendly and there won't be anyone very exciting there.'

But all the same, Nancy did take great care as she dressed, wearing a white frilly frock that Candy silently thought was an unfortunate choice for it made Nancy's hips look bigger than ever, but how did you tell her that without hurting her feelings? Then Nancy had tried a new kind of *home perm* on her hair and it had turned out rather frizzy. She dived excitedly on Candy's beauty-case and borrowed eye shadow and even some false eyelashes that Candy had bought for a joke but never had sufficient courage to wear.

Candy had chosen a simple scarlet frock with a tight bodice and a very full skirt. She brushed out her curls — for once she would not wear them in a chignon — and tied a scarlet ribbon round her hair in Alice-in-Wonderland style.

Nancy stared at her in some dismay. 'You look gorgeous but . . . but . . . most awfully young,' she said worriedly and then laughed. 'Not that it need worry you for you've got Andrew eating out of your hand.'

Candy flushed. It was not a nice expression. 'He isn't . . . '

'Isn't he . . . ?' Nancy asked and someone banged on the door.

'Bob is waiting for you — ' Matron called. Matron and Mrs. Combie had decided to stay at home, they preferred a quiet evening chatting together they said.

Everyone else was in the hall. Bob Robinson drove the two girls in his somewhat aged car and he drove fast but very well. Not as well as Dr. Faulkner, of course, Candy thought as she clung to the side of the car as it twisted and turned down the steep road.

As they passed the doctor's house near Nsingisi, Bob said: 'That's where Bill Abbott lives, Candy. They call him *Ebubesi* — the Africans do, I mean. It means *the lion*, because he fights and attacks the witch doctors . . . You should get him to talk one day, Candy . . . '

'I don't often see him,' she said. 'He pops into the office and out again.' Which was true for Bill Abbott had struck her as being a very elusive man. Maybe that was the secret of his bachelorhood!

The hotel at Nsingisi was decorated with great branches of red blossoms, bowls of deep blue flowers. Drinks were handed round and Bob introduced Candy to some of the local people, all of whom Nancy knew, of course. Dr. Faulkner and his sister, Candy saw, were sitting with a group of local people, and although he gave Candy a polite smile there was no warmth in it and she had a strange feeling of being snubbed. Had she been too impulsive over the chocolates, said something she shouldn't? The rest of the staff were either in groups or talking to friends round the bar and when the gong sounded, everyone made their way into the large dining-room where Bob again sat with Candy, who felt grateful to him for keeping her laughing all through the very good dinner of lobster salad, duck and green peas and fruit salad to follow. Despite her efforts to be cheerful, she felt strangely depressed — as one does when a cloud suddenly obscures the sun on a warm day.

After dinner, everything changed. Local young men came streaming in to the hotel and Bob introduced her to farmers, policemen, foresters, Civil Servants, who made a great fuss of Candy, dancing with her to the radiogram, giving her no time to sit and mope. She had left her glasses behind but no one commented. As she danced, she saw that Miss Faulkner was talking most of the time to a big white-haired man Candy had met, a Colonel Grant, ex-policeman now farmer.

Candy was dancing with a lean farmer who kept cracking jokes as they danced past Miss Faulkner and both were struck by the anger on her face. They looked at one another and then at the object of Miss Faulkner's obvious wrath and Candy saw that it was directed at Dr. Faulkner who was dancing with a very glamorous-looking blonde, whose hair was piled high bouffant style, three rows of pearls round her throat, diamond ear-rings swinging, bracelets jangling on her wrists.

Candy's partner whistled softly. 'That's Daphne — ' he told Candy as he whirled her round. 'Her child goes to your school. Poor little brat . . . '

Candy looked into the sun-tanned face. 'Because she goes to our school?'

He chuckled. 'No, because she is a poor little brat. She's the child of Daphne Arden's first husband. Daphne has just divorced her second husband and there is some talk of her re-marrying. Local gossip has it that she is after Dr. Faulkner but that his sister will never allow it . . . ' The music stopped and he led her out to the stoep, getting her a drink and then they sat on a sofa, gazing up at the enormous golden moon in the dark sky.

'Tell me — ' Danny said, smiling at her, his voice mischievous. 'It isn't true, is it, that Andrew engaged you in Durban? How did you escape being eaten alive by his sister?'

Candy stared at him in some dismay, for she thought that *joke* had been laid for ever. Besides it was disloyal to discuss your employers.

Danny guessed at her discomfort and chuckled. 'It's no secret that Constance is jealous and possessive and the last secretary . . . '

'Had a nervous breakdown,' Candy said firmly, trying to think of a way to change the conversation.

'Is that their story?' Danny asked, chuckling. His voice changed, became grave. 'I say, am I shocking you? You mustn't mind the way we gossip here. It's like living in a goldfish bowl. There is nothing to talk about but each other. It isn't as if we talked maliciously.'

Candy stared at him, looking very young and innocent. 'But how can you tell when it stops being fun and becomes malicious?' she asked.

He looked uncomfortable but changed the subject as a car arriving gave him the opportunity. 'The tall thin man with a serious face is Anthony Tester,'

Danny told Candy. 'He's a missionary out at Kubula.' She looked at the earnest man who walked as if he were quite alone, his face thoughtful. Behind him came a quietly-pretty girl with honey-coloured hair in a blue frock — she was almost running, her face eager as she hurried into the hotel. 'That's his sister, Dene,' Danny said in Candy's ear. 'She's a nurse. Rumour has it that she'd like to marry the doctor but . . . ' He went red as Candy turned to look at him. 'Sorry — ' he said and sounded uncomfortable. 'I forgot you don't like gossip. Ah — there is Bill . . . ' he said, sounding relieved, standing up as Bill Abbott walked in.

He came straight to them, smiling down at Candy, shaking Danny by the hand. 'Haven't seen you in years, old man. Hi — ' he said to Candy, 'Enjoying yourself?'

Danny laughed uneasily. 'I'm either boring or shocking her. It seems Miss White doesn't approve of gossip.'

Bill chuckled. He looked very handsome in his dinner jacket, his blond hair smooth, his dark-lashed eyes twinkling at Candy. 'It's hard to avoid it here . . . Mind if I steal her for a dance, Danny?' He smiled at Candy. 'Care to risk your life?' he asked, holding out his arms.

Candy was glad to escape from her companion and go back into the crowded room. He danced very well, holding her close, smiling at her flushed face and saying very gently. 'They don't mean to be unkind. It's just a bad habit small communities get into — that of gossiping.'

'I'm afraid I sounded like a prude . . . ' Candy confessed, 'But . . . ' she spoke with sudden earnestness. 'Gossip can be so cruel and . . . and it does seem such a tame excuse to say there is nothing else to talk about. There's books and plays and films and world events and . . . ' She paused for breath. 'In any case, why don't people mind their own business?'

He held her a little away from him and gazed down at her flushed face, frankly puzzled. 'Why,' he said slowly. 'You are really upset.'

She looked up into his good-looking concerned face. 'Please tell me,' she said very earnestly. 'Why does everyone seem so surprised that I got the post of secretary? Why can't a young person be just as efficient as an older one?'

Bill whistled softly. 'So that is what gets your goat! I didn't think you minded so much — ' He looked into her grey eyes and then whirled her round the room as he thought quickly. 'You see, Candy — ' he said as he slowed up again, 'the last secretary made a fool of herself.' He paused again as he saw Candy's frank surprise. 'She was very young — ' he went on, 'And rather a romantic type and she . . . she fell in love with Andrew Faulkner . . . '

Candy's face cleared miraculously. Now she understood! 'Oh poor girl,' she said at once. 'Of course she had to go. Bill . . . ' She flashed him a smile. 'Thanks for telling me. It explains a lot of things. Funny, though, for he's old . . . I mean, he's not young and romantic and . . . He's different . . . '

The doctor studied the earnest face for a moment, liking the way her soft hair curled, thinking how much more beautiful her eyes were without the fake glasses. 'Is he different?' he asked dryly.

'Oh yes, quite, quite different, Bill,' she said eagerly. 'You see, although he can be very kind and thoughtful and very appreciative — he gave me some chocolates the other day for working late — but he is also very formal. I can't imagine him . . . ' She gave Bill a swift friendly smile as she spoke: 'Giving any girl reason to think he was in love with her. I mean, he's so dignified . . . '

'I doubt if he did give her any reason,' Bill said, his voice dry. 'She was not the type of girl he would want to marry, and he is not the kind of man to . . . ' Bill said with a quick charming grin, 'philander, to use one of his sister's words. She was a romantic girl and wove dreams, that's all. Andrew is an impressive-looking man, but the pity is there need have been no gossip or talk at all if only . . . if only Constance had left well alone. As it was the poor girl had hysterics and landed up in hospital with a nervous breakdown. You see, Candy — this girl — Isobel Cartwright — was only twenty-three and everyone said that in future the Faulkners would choose an older woman, one not likely to be a romantic . . . ' he said, smiling down at her. 'Maybe they think you are too young to be romantic . . . '

'Can one be too young?' she asked him as he twirled her round and round the room her feet hardly touching the floor. Her hair bounced about, her cheeks were flushed as she laughed up at him. 'I have been in love several times, Bill, but somehow the affairs all died a natural death. Sometimes I got bored — sometimes they did . . . '

The music stopped and breathless, she went with him to a chair.

'Would you like a drink?' he asked.

'No thanks, I've just had one . . . ' Candy told him.

He looked across the room and she saw that the nurse — Dene Tester — was waving to him, her face bright with happiness. Bill hesitated but Candy said quickly, with one of her swift bright smiles.

'I'll be all right, Bill — Your friend is waving to you . . . '

He grinned. 'I know you'll be all right . . . ' he said, for the music was starting again. 'You'll have a partner in two shakes. Be seeing you . . . ' He lifted a hand in a farewell salute and strolled across the empty dance floor.

As Candy watched, she saw Dene come running to meet Bill Abbott, saw the way she held both his hands to greet him, then tucked her hand through his arm, smiling up at him and talking earnestly as they joined her brother. What was it Danny had said? That Dene wanted to marry Bill . . .

A deep voice said formally: 'May I have this dance?'

Candy turned her head and her heart seemed to do a most strange thing — as if it jerked. Dr. Faulkner was smiling down at her, his eyes warm and full of admiration. She stood up and went into his arms as if it was the most natural thing in the world.

6

The First Day

Candy moved stiffly round the floor in Dr. Faulkner's arms, dismayed and hurt for it was like dancing with a stick or a lamp-post. The whole experience had been like jumping into a warm pool and finding that it was filled with ice water. What had happened? She had been so sure that he liked her, would enjoy dancing with her. She had thought his eyes had admired her . . . but he was dancing like an automaton. Obviously this was a duty dance to be endured and got over as soon as was decently possible. Horribly deflated, she was tempted to tell him that he need not dance with her . . . The dance seemed never-ending and she was most uncomfortable. He was so tall and so stiff. Yet oddly when she had danced with Bill — who was even taller than Dr. Faulkner — she had not been conscious of the great difference in their heights. But maybe that was because Bill held her close and had also bent his head to talk to her as they danced . . . At last the music came to an end and it was a relief to move out of that stiff impersonal embrace.

Dr. Faulkner stared at her and blinked, as if seeing her for the first time. 'Enjoying yourself?' he asked in a kind voice, such as one would use to a child.

Candy lifted her chin and smiled at him. 'I'm having a lovely time, thank you,' and they walked silently to her chair.

She was sure he was relieved as she was when Danny, the young farmer, hastened to her side, saying he wanted to introduce her to some friends of his. As she walked across the empty floor with Danny, she turned her head to watch Dr. Faulkner and saw that he went straight to the side of Mrs.

Arden, the glamorous divorcee. Was there some truth in the rumour that he wanted to marry her? How would Miss Faulkner react? How would Mrs. Arden fit into the life of the school? Would she attempt to do so . . .

Candy's cheeks flamed. Why, she had nearly bitten poor Danny's head off for gossiping and now she was just as bad. She looked up at the thin young man by her side and said frankly: 'Danny, I'm sorry if I sounded horribly smug just now. I didn't mean to but Mummy has told me of so many cases where gossip got out of hand and ruined lives . . . ' She looked up at him earnestly: 'Mummy is a perfectionist and I had no right to preach at you . . . '

She was startled by the sweetness of his smile. 'That's all right, Candy,' he said at once. 'You were quite right. It is horribly easy to slip into the habit of talking scandal and it can ruin lives. Bill is a case in point. No one knows quite what is the mystery about his mother but the talk is quite shocking and a nicer man than Bill never lived . . . '

'I quite agree,' Candy said and then she found herself being introduced to Dene Tester, the girl in the blue frock, and liked her instantly.

'How are you settling down?' Dene asked, making room for Candy to sit down next to her.

'I'm loving it,' Candy said. 'Though until school really starts, I can't honestly say.'

Dene gave her a quick sympathetic smile. 'I don't imagine you could work much harder . . . '

Candy chuckled. 'No — it has been a bit grim.'

She was introduced to Anthony Tester who gave her a rather vague smile and said politely that he hoped one day she would come out and see the Mission. His eyes, deeply sunk in his gaunt face, glowed as he talked of it, he had a very small clinic, a school. Candy listened and found herself envying him for how wonderful it must be to know so plainly what you want to do with your life, and to have the courage to be able to do it.

Going home in the car, Candy dozed. She could hear Nancy giggling as Bob teased her but it was only when Nancy turned and said: 'I saw you dancing with Andrew . . . ' that Candy began to wake up.

'Just a duty dance . . . ' she said sleepily. 'And the poor man hated every moment of it.'

'H'm . . . ' Nancy said disbelievingly.

Candy woke up properly. Whatever happened, she did not want Nancy to start teasing her about Dr. Faulkner! 'Didn't he dance with you?' she asked.

'Oh yes . . . once,' Nancy admitted reluctantly.

'You see . . . ' Candy said. There was a lot more she wanted to say but decided the moment was not ripe.

The three were squashed in the front seat of the car and had to shout above the noisy engine as the car swung round corners, tearing down mountain roads . . . it was all something of a nightmare so Candy leaned back in her corner, closing her eyes and crossing her fingers and hoping for the best. It was a relief when they reached the school and could go indoors and tumble into bed. It had been a strange evening, with moments of pleasure but also some bad moments as well.

After the party, came two days of sheer hard work with hardly a moment to spare and Candy's fingers racing over the typewriter keys as she tried to keep pace with the work that poured in. It was a relief when one morning she awoke and knew the mad rush was over for that day, school began.

There was little conversation at the breakfast table and Candy wondered when the children would start to arrive, but afterwards Miss Rowland asked her to be prepared for the onslaught of the parents any time after twelve o'clock.

'Relax until then, Miss White,' she said in the formal voice she kept for working hours. 'Walk round the garden and then come in and pretty yourself up . . . ' She smiled at Candy. 'We must make a good impression on the parents, you know.'

'What will I have to do?' Candy asked, suddenly unsure.

Miss Rowland laughed. 'My dear child, don't look so terrified. Just what you have been doing all along. Helping us. Keep watching to see if any children arrive when the Faulkners and I are occupied with parents and then go and welcome them and explain that while we are engaged, we won't be long . . . and point out something . . . the roses or the swimming-pool — just keep them happy so that they don't feel neglected or ignored. All right . . . ?'

Candy's face had dimpled with laughter. 'Quite all right, thank you.'

Obediently she wandered round the lovely gardens and then strolled past the African quarters and paused to smile at the small African children, playing in the dust before the thatched mud huts. A few old 'grannies' came out to stare at her, huddled in saffron-coloured blankets despite the heat, and Candy realised with a shock that with such a large staff for the school — both indoors and out — most of the mothers and all the fathers who lived here must be employed by the Faulkners. The gardens were always kept looking beautiful and the school was polished and spotlessly clean, thanks to Mrs. Combie's clever administration.

At ten to twelve, she changed into the navy-blue shantung suit she had worn when Dr. Faulkner interviewed her, she brushed her hair back tidily and used a double lot of hairpins to make sure the chignon should not collapse, and then surveyed her face gravely in the mirror, pushing back the wretched spectacles that slid down her nose the whole time.

At twelve-fifteen exactly, the first car arrived and, hovering in the background, Candy watched Dr. Faulkner walk down the wide steps to welcome the first child and his parents. Almost at once, another large car slid up and there was Miss Faulkner, regal in palest mauve, smiling graciously, extending a hand of welcome to the elegantly-dressed couple who emerged, complete with two small, miserable-looking boys. Then another car and Miss Rowland was occupied and then a fourth . . . and Candy found herself going down the steps without any nervousness to smile at a tall plump girl who looked as if she had flung her uniform on in a furious temper and hated the world. Candy introduced herself to the harassed-looking mother and the father who looked really bad-tempered, and discovered the girl's name was Rosemary and that she hated school. It was not a very auspicious beginning for Candy too had hated boarding school for many reasons but when she sympathised, the girl looked as if she would burst into tears so that it was quite a relief when Miss Rowland took over with a firm: 'Ah,

Rosemary — the very girl I want to see. I want you to organise the play-readings this term . . . ' And Candy witnessed the miracle as Rosemary's miserable face blossomed into a beam of delight and her eyes glowed excitedly.

Candy retreated to a strategic position and realised there was more to welcoming the children back than merely standing there politely. Miss Rowland had the right 'touch', knew how to make a child feel important, to promise that life would prove interesting.

Gradually more and more cars arrived and departed, and the usually quiet garden and house seemed to be full of children of every age and appearance, with a lot of parents milling round, needing to be shown over the school. A few of the smaller children wailed when their parents left them but Matron and Nancy were in evidence to rescue the unhappy parents who hovered — not sure whether to beat a cowardly retreat or offer a bribe if only the precious child would stop crying — but very few children wept, and those who did, soon forgot it once their parents were out of sight, and most of the children seemed delighted to see one another and the place resounded with laughter and clumping footsteps.

Candy saw that she was no longer needed for now the rest of the staff were mingling with the throng, so she crept away to her office and sat by the window, in case some parents arrived and there was no one to receive them. Her head ached and she was appalled by the noise and excited voices and laughter which seemed to overflow as if the building could not hold all the children.

Looking out of the window, she saw Miss Faulkner looking round vaguely so she hurried to her side but Miss Faulkner merely frowned and told her to get on with the correspondence.

Thankfully Candy scurried back to her office. It was absurd to feel that the mass of children were overpowering.

Of course, normally they would be in different groups or classes, not all making a noise at the same time. She knew that certain of the more favoured parents were being given tea in the Faulkners' little house but that had nothing to do with her. Nor did the children. She felt thankful to be a little aloof from it. She knew she could never have been a school teacher . . . the mere thought was too appalling . . .

The door opened and Bill Abbott popped his head in. 'Hi — ' he said as usual. 'You're the lucky one. Well out of it. I suppose the Duchess is dancing attendance on the bread tickets?'

Candy could not help smiling though she felt it rather a crude way of putting it. 'I think they're giving some of them tea in their own house. Do you want to see her?'

Bill came into the room with his long easy stride and leaned against the window, staring out at the school bus that had just arrived and from which was pouring a stream of noisy boys

108

and girls. 'Not particularly but I must, sometime,' he said. 'Got a headache?'

'I have — rather,' she said, the abrupt question jerking the truth out of her.

He turned to smile at her, the sun glinting on his fair hair. 'Then pack up and come for a run in the car. I have to go over to the Mission,' Bill suggested. 'You won't be missed,' he added, guessing the reason for her hesitation.

'I'd love to, but . . . ' Candy said.

He grinned. 'I know. Look, I'll ask Philippa. I know she'll say it is okay . . . ' He disappeared through the door and she hastily finished the letter she was typing and put it in the wire basket. She was more than half-way through the letters and there was no real hurry. It would be lovely to get away from the noise and the heat — to feel the mountain air on her hot cheeks.

Bill came back, beaming. 'Okay. The Duchess is closeted in her house with a chosen few. Andrew is battling with a professor who knows how difficult children should be handled and Philippa says she envies you and no one will miss you. I'll bring you back in good time . . . ' he promised.

It was heavenly to pull the cover over the typewriter, tidy up and go out into warm fresh air with Bill. He had parked his car well away from the huge impressive-looking cars that stood in the drive, and in a moment, they were driving out of the gates.

'All the parents seem most frightfully wealthy — ' Candy said and Bill smiled. 'Why do you smile like that?' she asked.

He chuckled. 'For the simple reason that unless the parents are wealthy, their children can't come to this school. Haven't you read a prospectus yet and seen what the fees are?' he asked.

'No. I never thought of doing so — ' Candy admitted.

Bill drove fast but well and she relaxed happily by his side, feeling the wind through the open windows tugging at her once-neat hair.

Without looking at her, he said: 'Why not let your hair down for a change?' He chuckled at her face. 'You'll lose your hairpins if you don't . . . and do take off those stupid glasses that make you look like an owl.' He chuckled again. 'And that was meant as a compliment for owls have always been my favourite birds, especially very young owls with enormous eyes like yours.'

Candy smiled at him, obediently took out the hair-pins and ruffled her hair, and then tucked her glasses in her pocket. 'That's much better — ' she admitted and let her head rest against the seat, looking out of the open window at the four huts and a cattle kraal they were passing, hedged by brilliantly yellow flowers and then the car began twisting, turning and descending into the ravine Nancy hated. She loved the cool wind on her face, the feeling of her hair being tugged by a friendly hand.

'This is very nice,' she said happily.

Bill threw her a quick smile. 'Thanks. Nice because you are with me — or nice because it is preferable to working in that stuffy office?'

'Nice for both reasons . . . ' she said teasingly, laughing up at him.

She always felt completely at ease with Bill. He joked and teased and flirted mildly but it was in such a casually nice, friendly way that there was nothing too personal about it. Would he marry Dene? Surely a nurse was the perfect wife for a doctor? Dedicated, unselfish and, as Dene obviously was, adoring.

They had left the main road behind and were jolting over a very bad road, full of ruts and holes.

'Look — ' Bill said abruptly.

She followed his pointing finger and saw the small buck at the side of the road, standing tense, on his face a look of fear as he stared at them, and then he had bounded away and out of sight in the bushes.

'How lovely — ' Candy said, staring into the bush hopefully.

Bill nodded. 'We often see them round here. Beautiful animals but a bit of a nightmare to the Mission for they come down at night and eat all the young vegetables. What did you think of Anthony?'

'I hardly spoke to him,' Candy said slowly, she never liked giving spot-opinions of people. 'He was very interesting . . . '

'He's a fanatic,' Bill said curtly. 'Not always wise — or fair. Now Dene is quite different.'

'Is she?' Candy asked. Had his voice softened? 'She seemed very nice and friendly but you know how it is at a dance . . . you just talk polite talk.'

He smiled. 'How right you are. No, Dene is a very lonely girl. Anthony's life satisfies him completely but I still think she should have stayed in a big hospital. After all, if Anthony hadn't got a sister . . . ' He paused, negotiating an almost blind corner slowly. Far below them, Candy could see the valley, half-hidden in a mist haze. 'Dene needs companionship, the spur of emergencies, the hum of a big establishment. Here she is wasted. She has stabbings and a few broken heads to deal with but never anything really dramatic — and Dene thrives on drama — ' he said surprisingly, swinging the wheel of the car round sharply as they met another steep bend.

Candy stared at him in amazement. Drama was the last emotion she would have associated with Dene.

'Here we are . . . ' he said and he sounded so glad that she realised he had been longing for this moment.

They slowed up as they reached a few thatched buildings with a fence built round them. African children played outside a few small mud huts and from somewhere a baby wailed. They were high above the valley and the wind blew almost blusteringly, whirling up the sand, making the few slender trees bend. The sky was very blue and the sunshine very bright, and Candy thought the colours of the blanket round the shoulders of a very thin, bent old African who came out of one of the buildings to stare at them, dazzling.

Bill blew a gay fandango on the car hooter and almost instantly from behind the old man Dene came hurrying, looking thinner than ever in a blue frock with a starched apron. 'Bill . . . ' she cried gladly, and then something seemed to happen to her face as she saw Candy. In a moment, she had recovered and was smiling as she came forward to welcome Candy. 'How lovely to see you.'

Feeling a little uncomfortable, Candy got out of the car. Quite obviously Bill would have been more welcome had he been alone. She looked round her curiously. How very austere it was. But the view down the mountainside and far over the distant valley was breath-taking; all soft blues and hazy browns with an occasional gleam of silver that must be a river.

'How lovely it is here,' she said warmly.

'Oh, it's beautiful enough — ' Dene said almost curtly. 'Bill — ' she turned eagerly to the doctor. 'I'm so glad you've come for I'm really worried about Abner's broken leg. I still feel he should go to hospital . . . ' She took Bill's arm and began to lead him away.

'Come on, Candy,' Bill called. 'Come and see Dene's hospital.'

Candy hesitated for Dene's face had gone red. Was she angry?

'Call it a hospital!' Dene said bitterly. 'I can only apologise for it, Candy, but what can you do when there is just no money available? How we would manage without Bill, I don't know,' she said and smiled rather coldly at Candy. 'Come if you like but don't be disappointed . . . ' she said almost reluctantly.

7

The Doctor is Surprised

Candy was to see the small 'hospital' many times in the future but she never forgot her first impression of the dim cool building with the strong pervading smell of disinfectant. As she followed the others, she realised that both had already forgotten her. Candy stared at the number of small babies, either in makeshift cots of wooden boxes, many in their mothers' arms; there was a small African boy who stared at her with huge curious eyes and whose face was covered with running sores. There at the far end of the hut — she could see Bill and Dene standing at the bed on which lay an African, his leg splintered and hoisted in the air by a sort of Heath-Robinson type of harness.

Her first impression was of noise, babies crying, children quarrelling, the strong strong smell of disinfectant . . . Then Bill came to her and took her on a 'tour of inspection', telling her that the many babies were there because they so easily got an infection of the eyes. 'Luckily Dene has persuaded the mothers to bring them in before the witch doctors get at them,' he said, his hand lightly on her arm.

An African in a huge night-shirt and with his head bandaged so that it looked like a great white turban was handing round mugs of some liquid.

'In a fight?' Candy asked, smiling at her companion. Bill nodded. 'And how. They have brawls when they get drunk. The pity is that there is a good nourishing native beer that is perfectly suitable for them to drink but when they want to get an extra kick out of it, they add anything from fermented pineapples to methylated spirits.' He laughed at her look of horror. 'That's when the trouble starts.

They go berserk — are blind drunk and haven't a clue as to what they are doing. Dene gets a lot of broken heads and stabbings as a result. I often say their heads are made of iron for they come up smiling and probably will be back in a few weeks' time with another bad head. Isn't that right, Dene?' He turned to smile at the girl waiting so patiently.

'Quite right, Bill,' she said pleasantly but Candy recognised the note of repressed impatience in it.

'I'll leave you to your work — ' Candy said lightly, smiling at them both, and going outside into the bright sunshine, drawing in deep breaths of the mountain-fresh wind.

At that moment, the gaunt body of Anthony Tester emerged from another building. 'Ah — ' he said and sounded pleased. 'I am so glad to see you.'

He sounded as if he meant it. He was wearing khaki shorts and a bush jacket, his hair was rumpled and his cheekbones stood out. Was the man starving? Surely Dene would see to it . . . Or were they so very poor? Or was he the kind who couldn't find time to eat? Bill had said he was a fanatic.

'Bill brought me,' she explained. 'He's in the . . . the hospital with Dene.'

Anthony chuckled. 'Thanks for the compliment of calling it a hospital. Dene does wonders with very little. The trouble is she gets so vexed with the Africans — she can't seem to realise that they are just children . . . ' He sighed a little and then smiled. 'Like to see round the Mission?' he asked.

She was silent — and shocked — by the bareness of the little house into which he led her. Just sufficient furniture but no more. Shabby if comfortable chairs, a very old desk, bookshelves round the walls, filled with books that had obviously been read and re-read many times. The building was lofty with a raftered thatched roof, the walls were white. It was so very bare and clean and austere. Ideal perhaps for Anthony — but could Dene be happy here?

She stood at the window and stared admiringly at the peaks of mountains stretching away in the distance. 'It is like being on top of the world,' she said.

Anthony chuckled. 'Dene calls it the back of beyond. It is very good of her to stay here with me for she hates every moment of it. All the same . . . ' he said with another moment of gravity, 'Sometimes I wish she wouldn't. I hate to know she is unhappy . . . She feels so differently about it all . . . thinks I am just wasting my time . . . ' His face clouded for a moment as he stared at the view and then he brightened. 'Dene is the product of a London hospital. She likes order and sanity and knowing today what must be done tomorrow. In this sort of life you never know one moment to another what is going to happen. She has a constant battle not to lose her temper with her patients here. You give them *muti* — that's medicine — and if they don't like it, they call it *bad stuff* and pour it away — or they come in for a dressing on a wound and don't turn up for months and then return with a bland trusting smile and a terribly festering wound and you learn they've been 'treated' by the family witch doctor.' He sighed. 'Yet can you blame them? The family puts heavy pressure on them sometimes. They have terrific faith in their own doctors . . . '

He showed Candy the rather pitiful wind-swept garden with the neat rows of vegetables and the carefully weeded ragged flower garden. 'Why does Dene stay?' Candy asked.

'I was very ill,' Anthony said simply. Candy began to understand. 'Dene says that if she was not here to bully me, I forget to eat.' He smiled — an absurdly young smile. 'To be honest, I'm afraid I do. There are so many other and far more important things to be done.' He looked down at her. 'Care to see the school?'

'I'd love to,' Candy said, putting her hands to her hair which was being blown all over her face. Could she bear to live in a place like this? You had to be dedicated . . .

She found the school enchanting. A long narrow room packed with African children of every age. The hum of voices as they entered the building and the thin African woman with beautifully high cheek-bones and dark glowing eyes said something quickly and all the children, with a scraping of benches and shuffling of bare feet, stood up. Watching the missionary's face Candy saw the love on it as he told the children to sit down and then led Candy down the room.

'This is Miss Stella Dhlamini — ' he said. 'I don't know what we would do without her.'

Candy held out her hand. 'You've got a very big class . . . '

The African girl shook hands and there was a strange look on her face. Candy glanced at the missionary, wondering if she had done something wrong and saw that he was beaming approval at her.

'They are so willing to learn . . . ' the African girl said quietly.

'That must make it very satisfying for you,' Candy said. 'I always thought one had to try to hammer knowledge into a child's reluctant brain,' she added, laughing a little as she remembered the many conversations on the subject in the staff room.

'Ah — ' Stella Dhlamini said softly. 'But you see, with us, it is different. When a thing's hard to obtain, you value it more.'

Candy stared at her. 'I suppose you do,' she said thoughtfully.

'My sorrow is that no one here can play the piano — ' Anthony said abruptly. 'The children love to sing — and sing very well without music — but they love to hear the piano played. Sometimes a visitor . . . '

Candy turned to him, surprised. 'I can play.'

124

Anthony's face was bright. 'How wonderful — ' and in a moment Candy found herself sitting in front of an aged piano, staring at the yellow keys and wondering if she was quite mad. What would the children enjoy?

But Anthony had everything organised and was opening a hymnal.

'Can you play from sight?' he asked anxiously.

Candy wanted to laugh. She rarely talked about it but she had nearly become a professional pianist. She had loved music, had worked hard, and then, at thirteen, had broken her hand. It had healed but had a habit of getting tired when she used it too much. All hope of a career as a musician had been cancelled and somehow she had not minded very much. She had hated disappointing her mother, had been saddened by her sorrow for her, but in her heart Candy had always wondered if she was dedicated enough to be a musician and accept the long and many hours of practice.

As her fingers found the right keys, she went on smiling. It was such a very old piano and some of the keys went dead as you touched them, but she could hear the children's voices behind her, gloriously carolling and could see Anthony's happy face as he turned the pages for fresh hymns for her to play.

She stopped when her hand began to ache. She sat there, rubbing it gently, and saw that Bill and Dene had joined them. Both were staring at her and Bill looked startled.

'I didn't know you were a pianist,' he said.

She stood up, still gently massaging her hand, smiling at them, and told them of the career that might have been.

'Please don't feel sorry for me . . . ' she added, laughing at them gaily. 'It was a disappointment when I disappointed Mummy but I don't think I was really dedicated enough. You know, it's very hard work,' she said. 'I'm lazy. I play to enjoy myself.'

'And to give pleasure to others,' Anthony said warmly. 'I do hope you will come again . . . '

'Of course I will,' Candy promised. The children were all smiling at her. It was a wonderfully appreciative audience.

Outside in the sunshine, having said good-bye to Miss Dhlamini and the children, Bill kept glancing at his watch, but Anthony insisted on showing Candy the little church. It was as bare as the rest of the buildings. On the altar, were silver candlesticks and a cross and two vases filled with glowing deep red roses. There were rows of backless benches in the church.

'I wish you could come to a service,' Anthony said wistfully.

Candy looked at his lean tired face. 'I might be able to borrow one of the school cars,' she said. 'Dr. Faulkner wants me to pass my test so that I can drive for them and he might lend me a car . . . '

Anthony's face was illuminated. 'That

would be wonderful.'

'We must really go — ' Bill said impatiently.

After the farewells had been said and they were in the car, she remembered his look of surprise in the school.

'Why were you so amazed because I could play the piano?' she asked, twisting sideways on the seat to look at him.

He gave her a somewhat sheepish grin. 'Frankly you amazed me, Candy. You had always seemed so — so sort of flippant, gay, casual . . . It startled me to hear you draw such beautiful sounds from that ancient piano and then . . . then the way you behaved there. The compassionate look on your face in the hospital — your patience with Anthony — your nice manner with the school teacher . . . ' He gave a short laugh. 'Frankly, it wasn't in keeping with what I had thought of you.'

Candy sighed. 'Bill — ' she said sternly. 'I do wish you'd realise that a girl, at twenty-one, is an adult. I may love to dance and laugh, and I know I often run where I should walk, but I am not a child.'

'I'm beginning to think you are right,' he said slowly.

As the car travelled the twisting mountainous roads, Candy battled with her hair. She must not go back to school looking too dishevelled.

'Anthony does look ill — ' she said suddenly.

'He is ill,' Bill said grimly. 'But he won't admit it. That's why Dene won't leave him.'

'I gathered that. It's rather wonderful of her,' Candy said slowly, thinking of the bleak lonely life.

Bill still looked grim. 'She is quite a girl,' he said.

Candy looked at him again. So he was in love with Dene? Then was it Anthony who was the stumbling block?

They reached the school as the sun went down — a glowing orb in a sky of mother-of-pearl — palest rose, faintest streaks of green, warm glowing yellow. The mountains shimmered in the beauty.

'They are so lovely — ' Candy said wistfully.

As they reached the front door, Candy was putting on her glasses.

'Thank you, Bill,' she said, turning to him with one of her warm impulsive movements. 'I think they are both wonderful.'

He smiled at her, watching her jerk her glasses into place. 'We must do it again,' he said and she wondered why he stared at her so strangely.

Inside she found that it was as Miss Rowland had said — no one had missed her. The building seemed to vibrate to the hum of voices. Nancy was up to her eyes in work but Candy found Bob Robinson in the staff-room.

He got up when he saw her and brought her a chair. 'Where did you sneak off to, you lucky girl?' he asked. 'I was grappling with parents who eyed me with accusing eyes. Is it my fault, Candy, that I am so handsome . . . ?' he asked, twirling imaginary moustaches and making Candy dissolve into laughter.

It was like being in a totally different world, she found as the days passed. A school empty and a school full of children were two different things. Now life ran to a strict schedule and always there was a background of voices, laughter, the clattering of shoes on the polished floors, the slamming of doors, the shouts from the playing fields. Now the school always seemed to be full — the very walls seemed to be bursting with their contents. Nancy was full of moans because of the overcrowding, Matron was quiet and disapproving for now that school had begun, the staff ate meals with the children but Candy ate in Mrs. Combie's room, together with Nancy and the Matron. Each morning when the staff were gathered on the platform of the assembly hall, resplendent in caps and gowns, Candy would slip in behind the children and listen to Dr. Faulkner's resonant, beautiful voice as he read the prayers. Then there was always a tense hush as the letters were handed out and you could see how the children longed to rip open the envelopes but were not allowed to do so until they had left the hall. Then Candy would go along to her little office and get on with her work. There was always enough to do but no longer so much. As both Miss Faulkner and her brother taught, they were seldom to be seen and both acquired the habit of dictating letters on the tape recorder. In the afternoons, Candy would slip out into the garden and wander around, watching cricket or tennis, or standing to laugh at the antics of the younger ones in the swimming-pool. Sometimes she felt it was a strange position — she was part of the school and yet not a part of it; she was like an onlooker, standing outside. At night, it was more like the old days for the staff would gather in their sitting-room and talk over the day's troubles or humours, or compare the laziness and exasperating qualities of their pupils.

She was typing one morning when Dr. Faulkner came into her office, looking quite incredibly handsome in his dark suit, white shirt and grey silk tie. 'Can you be ready in ten minutes?' he asked curtly. 'I am taking you into Nsingisi for your driving test.'

Candy stood up hastily. 'I will be ready, sir,' she said meekly and hurried upstairs to her pleasant little bedroom, wondering why she felt so excited. Maybe it was because she saw so little of Dr. Faulkner these days — maybe just because it would be a change — maybe . . .

She changed into a clean yellow-striped cotton frock, jerking her glasses up on her nose, brushing out her hair for it got less untidy in the car like that than when it was in its precarious chignon. She snatched up a blue cardigan, changed her shoes and hurried downstairs again.

Dr. Faulkner was sitting in the passenger seat of the car. He smiled when he saw her quick look of dismay. 'I want you to drive in,' he said. 'It will give you confidence for your test.'

She smiled rather weakly and found herself trembling as she took her place. So long as she didn't muff the gears or stall . . . or . . . or anything.

She sat stiffly and tensely at first and then Dr. Faulkner began to talk to her, casually, slowly, asking her questions about books she had read, putting her — she realised later — at ease, for suddenly she found herself more relaxed, beginning to enjoy herself.

As they drove down the one main street of Nsingisi, Dr. Faulkner smiled at her and said. 'I needn't wish you good luck with your test, Miss White. You don't need it,' he said, flashing her a brilliant smile as he spoke.

8

Confidences

Dr. Faulkner introduced Candy to Nick Bright, the giant of a man with blue eyes, very short white hair and a gruff voice.

'I'll see you at the hotel after your test, Miss White,' Dr. Faulkner said and left her.

Candy eyed her companion a little nervously as she took her seat behind the wheel. He settled himself beside her and folded his arms, looking at her grimly.

'I'm prejudiced against women drivers,' he said, 'So it is not really fair that I should test you, but Dr. Faulkner particularly asked me to do so because he appears to have such faith in you.' He looked even more disapproving. 'Have you driven before — I mean, before you came out here?'

'Yes,' she said and told him of her experience in England. 'I was rather scared at first out here,' she admitted. 'I had never driven on such steep roads or such bad surfaces — ' She flashed him a nervous smile. 'But the more I drive here, the more confident I feel.'

He nodded. 'Just a matter of adjusting your ideas a little; to remember to change gears on corners and to use your gears as brakes on the hills — also to avoid thick dust or sand, remembering that a dry skid can be as bad as a wet one. Well — ' he said dismally. 'Let's get going . . . '

He gave her curt directions where she was to drive him and then followed the toughest half-hour of her driving life. He seemed to think of every difficult dodge there was, and sat all the time with that poker-face and cold eyes. Yet, in a way, Candy found it exhilarating. It had the same effect on her that Miss Faulkner's attempts to trip her up, always had. It acted like a challenge.

Suddenly she lost all nervousness and was merely determined to show this arrogant male that women can drive as well as men!

At the end of the test, he shook her hand.

'Congratulations,' he said and a smile creased his stern face. 'For a woman driver, you are exceptional, for just a driver, excellent. Full marks, Miss White.' Suddenly his blue eyes were dancing. She stared at him a little mystified by the change in his attitude. As if guessing her thoughts, he added: 'I'll confess something, Miss White. I was sure a pretty girl like you would turn on the charm and try to make me pass you on that score . . . ' He chuckled at her shocked look and his eyes twinkled again. 'I assure you, Miss White, I have often experienced that. As I feel very strongly about the need for good drivers, it always angers me.'

'It never entered my head,' she said honestly.

He laughed. 'I could see that — Now

drive me back to the hotel.'

Dr. Faulkner was waiting on the stoep of the hotel, reading a newspaper. He looked up with a smile. 'You passed, of course . . . '

Her cheeks glowing, eyes bright, Candy told him what Mr. Bright had said. 'I wasn't a bit nervous. It was a challenge.'

He smiled. 'I knew you'd be all right . . . '

'I think it was your confidence in me that gave me the courage,' Candy said impulsively.

He chuckled. 'You're too modest. Look, shall we have some lunch, here?' He glanced at his wrist watch thoughtfully. 'We could get back in time but it would be a rush . . . '

The pleasant unhurried meal was the perfect sequel to the exciting strain of the morning. Sitting alone with Dr. Faulkner at a small table in the corner of the dining-room, Candy forgot all about being dignified and 'older' and laughed and joked naturally, just as she would have done with Nancy and Bob. Maybe she was a little fey with excitement, maybe the uniqueness of the situation had gone to her head, but it wasn't until the end of the meal that she began to have misgivings. As they drank their coffee on the cool stoep, shaded from the sun by the thickly growing branches of the bougainvillaea, she said nervously:

'I'm afraid I talk too much . . . '

Dr. Faulkner stretched out his long legs comfortably and turned to look at her, lifting his eyebrows slightly. 'Please don't apologise for what has been a pleasant interlude.' He smiled at her. 'I get so tired of people being on their guard with me. I only wish we could do this more often, but it is a little difficult . . . '

He paused and she stared at him, a little startled. The handsome often stern face was relaxed. He looked at ease, happy.

He linked his hands behind his head against the back of the long wicker chair. 'It can be very lonely,' he said, 'Being headmaster of a school. All eyes are on you. If you are friendly with one person, someone else resents it — may even take it out on that person in revenge.' He sighed. 'If you enjoy someone's company you dare not show it in case you encourage gossip. I don't suppose you understand,' he said a little wearily.

Candy sat tensely, staring at him. She understood only too well. He was thinking of poor Miss Cartwright who lost her heart. 'I think I do,' she told him quietly.

He turned his head and gave her that swift brilliant heart-warming smile. 'I think perhaps you do. You have a sensitivity that most girls of your age lack.'

She blushed with pleasure. 'I — I can see that life must be difficult for you.'

He chuckled. 'A wonderful understatement. If only you knew . . . ' His face clouded for a moment. 'Drink up your coffee. Unfortunately we should be making our way back.'

He drove back — for he said he expected she was tired. She was glad to relax by his side. It was a strange journey for he talked all the time. It was as if some gate had been unlatched and the words poured out. Sitting close to him because the rush of the wind as they raced along the narrow mountainous roads made it difficult to hear, she listened in amazement.

'My sister and I don't always see eye to eye . . . Of course she is so much older . . . ' The sentences seemed to be flung at her as he stared straight ahead. 'A wonderful woman . . . difficult to understand . . . I owe her so much . . . My parents died when I was four years old . . . ' Candy stared at his beautiful hands as they rested on the steering wheel, masculine slender fingers with filbert-shaped nails. She tried to see him as a boy of four . . . 'My sister brought me up — sometimes is overpowering. I had a school of my own . . . don't suppose

you know that? It failed, of course . . . '
he said bitterly. 'Too many ideals and
not enough common sense. Then my
sister asked me to help her. I didn't
want to . . . don't believe in working
with relations . . . ' He smiled ruefully
down at the quiet girl by his side.
'Trouble is, I owe her so much. This
isn't my idea of how to run a school
but of course, she is right. We can't
afford to be philanthropists, can we?'

He slowed up as the car went down
the steep hill towards the cement
causeway over the river. 'Am I boring
you?' he asked.

'Of course you're not . . . ' Candy
said, turning to him eagerly. 'I . . . '

He was not listening. He seemed to
be talking to himself. 'It is so wonderful
to be able to relax. To be myself. Just
to talk to someone who understands,'
he said and his voice sounded quite
wistful.

He talked all the way back to the
school; talked of his troubles with the
staff, of his need to keep his sister

happy and yet put right some of the small things with which he strongly disagreed; of the difficulties of children with broken homes. As they reached the school gates and paused for them to be opened, he turned to Candy with a smile.

'I've been waiting for the opportunity to say this — why not throw away those stupid glasses?' he said surprisingly.

Candy's hand flew to her mouth in dismay. 'But . . . but . . . '

He chuckled as he drove slowly down the drive. 'My dear girl, they never fooled me for one moment. You wore them to get the job? I thought so.' He chuckled again. 'It wasn't the glasses that got you the job. They make you look younger, if anything, and very vulnerable. Besides it is most irritating to watch you constantly push the wretched things up on your nose all the time.' The car drew up outside the school and he turned sideways in the seat to smile at her. 'Throw them away. Constance will never notice. She is most unobservant and so long as you do your job as well as you do it now . . . ' He smiled again. 'And let your hair hang loose like this . . . ' He touched her soft dark curls lightly, an odd expression in his eyes. 'It's much prettier this way . . . '

Somehow, Candy got to her bedroom and stood in front of the mirror, staring in amazement at the reflection of the pretty girl with starry eyes and flushed cheeks, whose dark curls were wind-blown into glorious confusion.

'It's much prettier this way . . . ' He had said that. He had said he wished they could have lunch together more often. He had said . . .

She lay on her bed, kicking off her shoes, wriggling her toes, stretching her body luxuriously. It had been a wonderful day. The nicest she had ever spent. The challenge of the driving test — and then the surprisingly pleasant lunch — and the way Dr. Faulkner had confided in her . . .

It was impossible not to have been

flattered. That he should trust her . . . like her sufficiently . . . She could not believe it. What made him change so suddenly? Hither-to, although he had always been politely friendly, there had always been a formalness about his behaviour that was unmistakable — a sort of barrier that it had felt impossible to cross. Yet now . . .

Yet in the days ahead, it was as if the little episode had never been except when he would suddenly glance at her directly across the room, or he would give her a quick significant smile. Small unimportant moments yet they seemed to link them in a new way; she had the feeling that he was asking her to understand something.

Taking his advice, she had left the glasses off and no one, not even Miss Faulkner, commented. A few days later, she stopped brushing her hair back severely and torturing it into the chignon and just brushed it out naturally. Again, no one save Nancy, who gave Candy a little lecture on looking too young like that, commented. Slowly Candy began to wear her gay clothes, finding again that Miss Faulkner, who was also preoccupied these days, did not even notice.

And through all the days ran the thread of Andrew Faulkner and his changed behaviour. She could have understood another man talking to her like that, but Dr. Faulkner was always so self-contained, so controlled, that it was hard to imagine him feeling the need to *let down his hair*! Yet it was easy to understand what he meant by his 'loneliness'. However much he needed a sympathetic ear, he still had to be careful; especially, poor man, after the little episode of the secretary who had fallen in love with him. Oddly enough, now Candy began to understand better how it had happened. Her whole conception of Dr. Faulkner had suddenly changed. Before he had been an awe-inspiring, kindly, god-like sort of person. Now he was a human being, with troubles and problems of his own, someone much nearer her own level.

Candy was in Miss Faulkner's office one early afternoon, taking a letter down in shorthand when Dr. Faulkner walked through the room. He paused to say: 'Excuse me for a moment, Constance. I meant to ask you before, Miss White,' he said in his most formal tone. 'How is your mother?'

Candy, confused by Miss Faulkner's look of annoyance, said quickly.

'Oh, thank you, she's very well and happy. She is working hard, of course, but enjoying it all very much . . .' Candy paused. Her nervousness always made her talk too much!

'Good,' Dr. Faulkner said curtly. Then added. 'When are we going to have the pleasure of meeting her?'

'I'm afraid I don't know, sir,' Candy said, looking up at the tall man who towered above them, his face casually interested. 'Mother had hoped to come when she was lecturing in Durban but

147

she says her time there was so packed with lectures that . . . ' Again she was talking too much and too fast. Miss Faulkner was frowning heavily, tapping on the desk with an impatient hand. 'She has promised to come, sometime,' Candy finished her sentence.

'Good,' Dr. Faulkner said curtly. 'I look forward to meeting her . . . ' he said and left the office.

'Where had I got, Miss White . . . ?' Miss Faulkner snapped and Candy bent over the outlines in her notebook, wondering why she felt so dazed, so confused. It had been a simple question he had asked and yet . . .

It was a few days later that Dr. Faulkner approached Candy and asked rather apologetically if she would have time to sort his coloured slides and put them in their correct files.

'I usually show them to the school each term and I'm afraid they got somewhat muddled at the last lecture . . . ' he said, pausing at her desk.

'I'll be glad to — ' she said eagerly,

smiling up at him, her hands poised over the typewriter keys.

She saw the quick way he glanced at the closed door leading to Miss Faulkner's room and then he bent forward and said very quietly. 'I'm glad you took my advice . . . '

'Your advice?' she echoed rather stupidly, not understanding.

He smiled. 'About your hair — and your glasses.'

'Oh — ' she said, understanding now. 'No one has said anything.'

He laughed softly. 'I knew they wouldn't. People are absurdly blind at times. Besides Constance has accepted you. I think you have achieved something, there . . . ' His voice was still low, intimate, enclosing them for a moment in a small world of their own. 'She thinks highly of you — ' he said, now his voice slightly surprised.

'I'm . . . I'm glad . . . ' Candy murmured, a little confused. Miss Faulkner had said nothing of the sort to *her*. Indeed only that morning,

she had found fault with some typing
Candy had done, saying that it was time
a new ribbon was in the typewriter, and
had she to make so many erasures. As
there had been only one — and the
ribbon was less than two weeks old,
Candy had known the criticism was
invented to 'keep her in her place'.

She looked up nervously at the tall
man. He was hovering. No other
word. She wished he wouldn't — for
supposing Miss Faulkner walked in?

'Where shall I find the slides?' Candy
asked him, her body tense as she waited
for Miss Faulkner's door to open.

'I'll leave them in my study — ' he
told her. 'I'll be out all the afternoon if
you like to work in there. I'll set up the
projector and everything.' He paused. 'I
wish . . . ' he began.

Startled, she gazed up at him. Why
was he staring at her like that?

Then he said almost curtly, 'Never
mind . . . ' and walked out of the
room.

She was shocked to find herself

trembling as she began to type. Now why . . . What on earth . . . Yet why had he looked at her like that? What was it he *wished*?

She enjoyed her afternoon's work in Dr. Faulkner's study. It was quiet and cool and everything was ready for her. There was a small projector into which she put the slides to see what category they came under.

Some were of Africa generally, the Victoria Falls, the Kariba Dam, the fishing villages of the Cape — others were of England, the glorious Lake District, the Changing of the Guard. Many were of wild animals and these interested her most — the long necks and haughty eyes of the giraffes staring at the camera, the frightening bulk of elephants, the grotesque ugliness of hippos yawning in the river with tiny white birds standing on the huge grey heads.

Dr. Faulkner walked into the room just as she was tidying up.

'Have you finished them?' he said,

sounding surprised.

Candy looked up with her quick eager smile. 'Oh yes, and I did enjoy doing it. I do hope you will give a lecture this term on the wild animals. Where does one see them? I know there are monkeys in the trees by the river but . . . '

Something of Dr. Faulkner's tired look vanished. 'They were taken in the Game Reserves. You've never been to one? Of course not, how could you . . . ' He paused, frowning thoughtfully. Then he looked up and his face was suddenly bright. 'I — I'm taking some of the children to the Reserve this term.' He stared at Candy, his eyes narrowing thoughtfully. 'I wonder . . . if I could so arrange it, would you like to come with us?'

Candy clasped her hands together, staring at him grey eyes wide.

'Oh, Dr. Faulkner, if only I could . . . ' she said eagerly. 'Oh, it would be too wonderful for words. Do you really see lions and . . . and elephants and ... and things just walking about ... ?'

He chuckled. 'Especially *and things*,' he said. 'Their camouflage is so good, that they are quite hard to find at times. It isn't a very good season for going to the Game Reserves but we should still see plenty of wild animals. I'll see what can be arranged.'

Candy's eyes shone with excitement. 'It would be wonderful.'

He stared down at her. 'Don't talk about it — yet,' he said and it seemed to her that he lost his natural friendliness and retreated into his old formal self. 'Thank you for doing the slides for me,' he added almost curtly.

Murmuring a polite rejoinder, Candy slipped out of the room, wondering what she could have said to make him change like that. One moment, so easy and relaxed — the next stiff and formal.

9

He Called Her 'Candace'

As great black clouds massed in the sky, with every now and then a jagged zigzag flash of lightning piercing the blackness, Candy constantly gazed out of the windows apprehensively for, though she hated to admit it, she was terrified of thunder storms.

'You'll get used to them here,' Nancy said cheerfully. 'We've been lucky so far but we are due for a spell of storms and rain.'

Candy's life at the school had settled into a regular, not unpleasant rhythm now, and often she had to drive into Nsingisi and enjoyed doing it. She also went the rounds with Nancy in the evenings and gradually got to know some of the children.

Molly Broom, the daughter of the

glamorous Mrs. Arden, was the problem child of the school. Angular, plain, with straight hair and glasses, she hated everyone.

'Can you blame her?' Bill Abbott asked bitterly one day. He had been called in to stitch up a deep cut on the girl's arm, caused when she thrust her arm through the bathroom window in a rage because she didn't want Nancy to wash her hair.

They were in Mrs. Combie's sitting-room, drinking the tea she had made him and Bill looked round at them all — at Nancy's flushed angry face, for she had been very frightened; at the Matron's little frown of worry, Mrs. Combie's always placid smile and Candy's unhappy eyes. 'Wouldn't you hate the world — ' Bill asked passionately, 'If you had a mother who can't be bothered with you? Who openly called you the Ugly Duckling? Who hasn't time to listen to your troubles but leaves you always with African servants? Wouldn't you hate the world when you saw your mother with different men and never knew from one day to the other what sort of step-father you might get next?'

He stood up and said good-bye to them all rather curtly. After he had gone, Nancy said, her voice a mixture of irritation and anxiety:

'It's all very well for Bill to talk but I have to look after her. She won't do a thing she is told without a battle first . . . '

Matron sighed. 'I know, dear, that it is very difficult for you. I think I'll put her in charge of her dormitory . . . '

Nancy stared in horror. 'She'll be impossible.'

Candy accepted another cup of tea from Mrs. Combie with a quick smile at her, brushed back her dark curly hair and said gravely: 'I think Matron is right, Nancy. We had a girl like that at our school, hating everyone and twice she was expelled and only taken back because the headmistress was sorry for her. They made her a prefect one day and from then on, she completely changed.'

'Because someone had confidence in her,' Mrs. Combie said quietly. 'No one loves or believes in Molly, poor child.'

'We'll try it,' Matron said firmly, and smiled at Nancy. 'Give her a chance, Nancy, and don't expect miracles straight away. She has got to adjust herself to being on the other side of the fence . . . ' she added with a chuckle.

Candy hurried down to her office. The mail was expected and she had to sort it. As she passed the music-room, she saw that the door was ajar and the room empty. On a strange impulse, she slipped inside, closing the door and — opening the piano — she began to play softly. She had not realised how much she had missed their own piano until the day she played at the Mission. Now, as she let her fingers wander idly over the keys, she dreamed a little — though she was not sure of what she was dreaming. The room was dark with the massed clouds in the sky and she shivered a little as if a chill wind blew.

With a shock, she remembered the mail that had to be sorted and she jumped to her feet, closing the piano, turning . . .

And in the same moment, she saw that Dr. Faulkner was standing just inside the door, looking at her with a strange expression on his face and there was a blinding flash of lightning and a terrific clap of thunder.

Things happened so swiftly that Candy never knew how it was that she found herself in Dr. Faulkner's arms, clinging to him, burying her face in his chest. He held her close as the ground seemed to be rocked by another crashing thunder-clap . . . and then the silence surrounded them and she made an effort to get control of herself. He knew the moment she had done so and his arms fell away. She stared up at him, her

158

small face drained white, her eyes enormous.

'I'm so sorry . . . ' she said, her face hot with shame. Supposing he thought . . . ? 'I didn't mean . . . I didn't know I . . . Oh, I am so sorry,' she added, horribly confused because he still said nothing but just went on staring down at her.

Then he spoke. A little formally. 'It is quite all right. I am well aware it was an automatic reaction.' He smiled at her and she felt even more confused and added: 'You are frightened of storms?'

She was still shaking and her knees felt absurdly weak and without thinking, she put out her hand. He took it, then took her other hand as well and held them both in his warm clasp as he gazed down at her. His voice was very gentle as he said:

'Look, try to remember that if you can see the lightning and hear the thunder, you are safe. It would be over before you knew it had happened . . . '

She tried to smile. 'I know. It's just
. . . just . . . '

'I know,' he agreed reassuringly.
'Now you must promise not to laugh if
I tell you something?' He smiled at her.
'I'm afraid of spiders.' He chuckled.

She could not help smiling. Spiders!
Some of the tension left her. Again and
again the gloom of the room was split
asunder by vivid flashes of lightning
and the air shaken by the blasts of
thunder but she no longer minded.

'I'm glad I'm not the only one with
fears,' she said.

He gave her hands another reassuring
squeeze and then let them go. He
leaned forward and whispered: 'I'll
tell you another secret. My sister is
scared of worms! Ordinary harmless
little worms.' He chuckled, his face
creasing with laughter. 'When I was
a child — a horrible little monster I
must have been — my favourite trick
was to drop worms down her back.
Did I laugh when she screamed!' He
smiled at her. 'Very shocked?'

160

Candy was herself again. Now she could laugh up at him, could push back her hair with one of those quick impatient gestures she had once used to push back her now-discarded spectacles. 'I think most people are shocked as they look back on their childhood.'

The tall, impressive-looking man with the smiling eyes was suddenly grave, as he said: 'How right you are. You say the most amazingly shrewd things sometimes . . . ' He smiled down at her as he added: 'Out of the mouths of babes . . . but I forgot . . . ' His eyes were twinkling. 'You are rather sensitive about your age. *I am twenty-one and Dr. Faulkner interviewed me . . .* ' he said teasingly.

Candy's face burned painfully. 'Some-one told you?' she gasped.

He laughed outright. 'Of course. We have our own grape vine whether we want it or not. I believe you were teased a lot when you came? I am sorry but I'm not sorry I took a chance and engaged you. I think we are very fortunate to have you . . . ' He glanced at his watch and looked dismayed. 'I must go. I have a meeting of the prefects . . . ' As he turned, he looked back at her. 'You are all right, now?' he asked and, when she nodded, added quietly: 'I wonder if you have any idea what a comfort you are to me.'

'Comfort?' Candy echoed, startled.

The handsome man smiled at her. 'Yes. You are the only person here with whom I can relax,' he said, and then he was gone and the door closed.

After a few moments and still feeling a little dazed, Candy went down to her office and saw the mailbag waiting for her. It was wet. She saw with surprise that the rain was beating madly against the window. It was as if the skies had opened and the rain came teeming down, falling fast and furiously so that the mud splashed up from the earth as the rain hit it.

As she sorted the mail, her thoughts roamed. What was it about her that 'comforted' Dr. Faulkner, helped him to relax? Everyone admired him. He was *different*, set apart from ordinary people. Yet he could be so gentle — so humble. How many men in his position would admit to be scared of spiders? She smiled. Poor Miss Faulkner and the worms. Imagine Dr. Faulkner as a horrid little boy, dropping worms down his sister's neck!

There were some letters on her desk to be done for Miss Faulkner. When she had finished them, she looked round carefully. Miss Faulkner still loved to jump on her if she had the chance. Taking the staff letters with her, Candy found it dark in the hall, the rain making an unceasing hissing noise as it fell.

Passing the open door of the Junior Playroom, she saw the children standing by the windows, gazing miserably at the rain and the ground fast becoming a quagmire.

'Isn't it a shame, Miss White?' Jenny Grace, an engagingly pretty child, said. 'It was the day for the tennis tournaments and look at the weather!'

Candy had forgotten about it. She knew how much it meant to them all. She looked at the young dejected faces and saw that, at one end of the room, there was a piano. 'Look,' she said impulsively. 'Why don't we have an informal dance? I'll play for you.'

Molly Broom's eyes were, as always, hostile. 'Can you play *modern* dance music, Miss White?' she asked.

'I'm not quite as old as that, Molly,' Candy said laughingly. 'I can play rock and roll, and bepop, and charleston, if that's what you like.'

Molly's face changed. 'I'm sorry. I didn't mean . . . ' she apologised awkwardly.

Candy laughed. 'I'm sure you didn't. I must seem frightfully old to you . . . '

Soon she had the children all dancing, many singing happily, their disappointment temporarily forgotten.

Candy did not hear the door open but she wondered why suddenly everyone stopped singing . . . Turning her head as she sang alone, she was startled to see Miss Faulkner standing in the doorway, her face furious.

'A little less noise, *please*, Miss White,' Miss Faulkner said in an icily cold voice and turned to leave the room.

There was an appalled silence. Candy pulled a rueful face and smiled at the children. 'I suppose we were making rather a noise,' she admitted.

'It was fun, though,' Molly said, her face bright and eager.

The children came to stand round Candy, all saying the same and thanking her.

'Why don't you just play to us, Miss White,' Jenny suggested. 'She couldn't object to that — ' she added rather scornfully.

'That's right,' Ernest, a too-tall, too-thin boy said. 'And play something *good* — not just jazz,' he said.

'We want jazz . . . ' the others shouted excitedly.

'I'll give you something of each,' Candy promised and proceeded to play until the jangling clanging of the bell called them all to tea and they trooped noisily out of the room.

Upstairs Candy remembered Miss Faulkner's anger and then forgot it as Nancy came bursting in, her face flushed.

'What do you think, Candy — ' she cried in a voice of despair. 'We've got measles. Matron has sent for Bill to come back but I doubt if he'll get through in this rain. It's just teeming down.' She went to the window and gazed out miserably. 'Of all things — to have rain and measles together!' she said explosively.

Candy suddenly remembered that she had left the staff letters on the piano downstairs! It was considered an unforgivable crime! She hurried down and found to her relief the letters as she had left them. As she took them with her and crossed the hall again, she met Miss Faulkner and her brother.

'Miss White — ' Miss Faulkner said in her iciest voice. Candy's heart sank. She clutched the letters, fearing Miss Faulkner's comments. 'Yes, Miss Faulkner,' she said very politely.

'Who told you to entertain the children in such an unseemly manner, Miss White?' Miss Faulkner demanded.

Candy stared. *Unseemly? Children?* 'I . . . ' she began as she grasped that Miss Faulkner could only mean the dancing and singing.

Dr. Faulkner interrupted her, his voice smooth. 'I asked Candace to play for the children,' he said quietly. 'I knew they were disappointed because the weather had stopped the tennis tournament.'

Candy stared at him. He was protecting her — and he had called her Candace!

'I am very sorry if we were noisy, Miss Faulkner,' Candy said placatingly.

'I hadn't realised we . . . '

Miss Faulkner's face was distorted with anger. 'Surely you are aware that I do not approve of such dances?' she asked frigidly. 'Rock and roll . . . ' She said the words as if they disgusted her. 'Waltz and some square dancing, or Scottish reels is a very different matter . . . '

Candy flushed. 'I am sorry, Miss Faulkner,' she said again. 'I didn't know you disapproved . . . '

Once again Dr. Faulkner intervened. 'How could she know, Constance?' he asked impatiently. 'We haven't had a dance since she has been here. In any case, I cannot think why you are so against rock and roll . . . '

'Andrew — ' Miss Faulkner said sharply. 'We have discussed this subject many times and . . . ' Suddenly it was as if she remembered Candy was standing there for she turned to her and said: 'That will be all, thank you, Miss White — ' Her voice was curt. 'Please do not let it occur again.'

'No, Miss Faulkner,' Candy said with outward meekness and escaped with relief, inwardly seething with wrath. How dared Miss Faulkner speak to her like that . . . And then her anger dissolved into warm happiness as she remembered that Andrew Faulkner had said: *Candace*. Was that how he thought of her?

* * *

As soon as she got the opportunity, Candy thanked Dr. Faulkner for his protection.

'I'm afraid I never thought I was doing anything wrong,' she told him, her eyes shining. 'I wanted to cheer the children up . . . '

He smiled and rested his elbows on his desk. 'Your motives were completely sincere and well-intentioned,' he said in the slightly pedantic manner he sometimes used. 'Unfortunately my sister is very intolerant and is convinced that rock and roll and vice go hand

169

in hand.' He smiled at the young girl sitting there with such an earnest look on her face. 'We know differently, of course. Unfortunately last term we had a bitter and rather publicised quarrel on the subject. It was not a happy occasion and Constance was ill as a result. Nowadays I try to avoid such occasions.'

'I am sorry,' Candy said slowly, staring at him. 'If I had known . . . '

'How could you know?' he asked and offered her a cigarette. He stood up and came to her to light it for her and his hand rested lightly on her shoulder. The touch of his fingers seemed to burn through the thin silk of her frock. 'Constance . . . ' he went on as he returned to his chair. 'Is a strange mixture. Full of common sense, a good organiser, clever with money but she has some blind spots. We do not see eye to eye about the way to handle children. You remember that you said you thought most adults looked back on their childhood and were horrified as to the way they had behaved? Well, I always try to remember my own youth when I handle young people. Constance, now, sets a standard of perfection that I am sure she never attained herself.' He smiled at Candy. 'She is fourteen years older than I am so I can't remember her childhood, of course, but I'm sure no human child could have been so perfect.'

'You told me once that you had your own school.' Candy ventured to say.

He stretched out his long legs and relaxed in the chair, looking thoughtful. 'Yes. I and an old friend went into partnership and started a school in the Highlands of Rhodesia. We were both idealists. The pupils were to be friends of ours. They were to learn because we made it so interesting that they would be unable to resist learning.' Andrew Faulkner smiled wryly. 'Well, that part was fine and we got wonderful results. Unfortunately we had a lot of friends who could not pay our fees but had promising children and we rather foolishly thought they would be a good advertisement for the school so we taught them for reduced fees.' He laughed. It was a short sharp bitter bark. 'We were very naïve. Things got worse and worse and then my partner walked out on me. It was a battle straightening things out but in the end, I sold the school. I was very depressed. Then Constance appealed for my help. She said she had the chance to build up a fine school but she needed me. Well . . . ' he said slowly, looking troubled as he stubbed out his cigarette. 'I have never been very happy working with her but she had always done so much for me that I felt I owed it to her. My dream . . . ' His face changed and he looked young and wistful for a moment . . . 'is that one day when this place is fully established I plan to sell my share in it and start on my own again.' He had been studying his linked fingers. Now he looked up at Candy with a quick friendly smile. 'Have you no idea when your mother is coming to see us? I do want her honest opinion of our endeavour.'

'I'm afraid I don't know when she is coming,' Candy admitted. 'She is so very much busier than she expected she would be . . . '

'You and your mother are very close?' Andrew asked thoughtfully. 'You have no father?'

Candy looked troubled, now. 'I'm afraid I know nothing about him,' she confessed. 'I don't know if he is dead or they are divorced. I only know it always upsets Mummy if I ask questions about him so . . . so nowadays I don't.'

'I see . . . ' Andrew said slowly. 'You are the only child?'

Candy nodded. 'Not that I've ever missed having brothers and sisters,' she added hastily. 'Mummy has always been wonderful to me. She has never denied me anything. I think I am very spoiled.'

'I think so, too . . . ' a grim cold voice said.

Candy turned instantly and Andrew looked up. Both stared in amazement at the angry woman who stood in the doorway.

10

A Kiss to Remember

Ten minutes later, Candy was back in her own office, cheeks red, heart pounding with anger. How dared Miss Faulkner be so insulting? Suggesting that Candy had neglected her work! And Andrew had stood up to her, had said Candy — only he had called her Candace — had been working for him and that she had not been there long. If it wasn't for Andrew, Candy decided, she would leave. Why should she put up with Miss Faulkner's rudeness . . . And then, suddenly, anger left her and she could be sorry for poor Miss Faulkner, embittered, narrow, jealous. Andrew had called her *Candace*, again!

Her fingers began to fly over the typewriter keys and even though the rain was beating wildly against the window and the skies were still dark and threatening, Candy felt like singing.

She had finished the letters when a fair head came round the door and Bill came strolling into the room.

'You look busy,' he commented; looking ruefully out of the window he added. 'What weather! I put chains on to get here and the roads are ghastly.'

'How are the measles patients?' Candy asked cheerfully.

He shrugged. Leaning his long thin body against the wall, he lighted a cigarette and smiled at her. 'As well as can be expected, I'm afraid.' He gave a rueful grin. 'You know, Candy, this school is understaffed at the best of times but when we get an epidemic like this, things really get out of hand. Nancy is showing signs of the strain and even Matron, bless her, admits that she is just a wee bit tired.' He smiled bitterly. 'I only wish I could make the Duchess realise how understaffed we are but all she can think of is the profit and loss account on the books.'

Candy was startled by his unusual bitterness. She realised guiltily that she had not noticed that Nancy was working so hard.

'Perhaps I could help . . . ' she suggested.

He grinned. 'Don't you work hard enough as it is?' Then he sobered. 'Perhaps you could help out at nights? There's no real nursing to be done, just to have someone on duty.'

'I'll ask Matron,' Candy promised.

Bill smiled at her. His eyes were twinkling and then as she stared at him, she saw the laughter vanish as he said: 'You like Anthony Tester?'

Startled, Candy nodded. 'I took Nancy over there the other Sunday.'

'I know. Anthony told me and you played for them again. Well . . . ' he said and sighed heavily. 'We've had to rush him to hospital with a haemorrhage. Frankly, I'm not too happy about him.'

'I am sorry. Poor Dene . . . ' Candy said at once.

'She is running the Mission for him for she knows that will help him most. He does worry so. I was only thinking, Candy, that when you are next in Nsingisi, that perhaps you could drop in at the hospital and see him. It would mean a lot to him. He likes you . . . though I'm sure I don't know why,' he teased, his eyes merry for a moment.

'I'm glad he likes me.' Candy said soberly. 'I admire him so much.' She doodled with a pencil, not meeting Bill's eyes. 'I also envy him. I mean, having a vocation like that. Knowing what you want to do and doing it.' She looked up at him, startled by a sudden thought. 'But then, Bill, you are like that, too. You have a vocation.'

Bill looked embarrassed. 'Oh, that's making it sound too noble. I just do a job of work,' he said uncomfortably.

Candy went on staring at him. It was as if she saw him for the first time. This tall, thin man with short blond hair, the hazel eyes, framed by long dark lashes, the stubborn chin and surprisingly gentle mouth. Why, Bill was quite someone, now she came to think of it. He was always so gay and flippant that she had been inclined to take him for granted, to think his life was an easy one. As Anthony had said once, Bill was always fighting. Ignorance, indifference, witch-doctors and then there was the mystery of his mother.

The door to Miss Faulkner's study opened. 'Miss White . . .' Miss Faulkner began curtly but she paused as she saw Bill and her face changed as she smiled at him warmly. 'Have you come to report on the progress of the patients?'

'Yes,' Bill said briefly and, with a lazy smile at Candy, followed the tall austere figure into the other room.

Left alone, Candy stared at the keys thoughtfully. Poor Anthony. But how could she get into Nsingisi? The roads were appalling; thick mud, slush, cars having to be dug out of it. She had never driven in mud. And then she knew what she could do. She would ask Andrew to take her with him the next time he drove into Nsingisi. Andrew did not mind mud!

Later Candy sought out the Matron. 'I wondered if I could help at night?'

Matron sighed. 'Well, you need your sleep, too, but . . . well, suppose you took over from eight o'clock in the evening for six hours . . . that would give us a chance to sleep and I'd let you sleep later in the morning for you could breakfast in bed.' She sighed again. 'Three of the staff are down with it now. Miss Stromberg considers it an insult that spots should appear on *her* body.' Matron chuckled for a moment. 'Bob, too, has been very sick but Nancy says he is better tonight. You wouldn't have to do any actual *nursing*, Candy, but it would be a great help. You're sure you don't mind.'

Candy laughed. 'Of course I don't mind . . . ' she said.

But much later that night, she

wondered if it was the truth. It was surprisingly hard to stay awake; she battled with sleep, her eyes closing, her head nodding whenever she sat down. She wandered constantly from ward to ward, trying to keep awake, pulling up the covers round Don Ackroy's neck, getting Michael a drink of water, telling Ernest the weather was changing, soon be cricket again, looking in on Bob, finding him sound asleep, a vase of rain-drenched roses on his table.

She sat in Matron's room, with a small lamp glowing but she felt on edge and absurdly nervous. It was eerie to be the only one awake in the quiet school. She stared out of the window at the dark night and saw that the dark clouds were rolling away and a small moon beginning to gleam.

She jumped at the sound of a footstep and swung round. It was only Kwido, one of the houseboys, with a tray of coffee. He gave a big grin, said it was Matron's orders and then padded away, his white jacket and shorts making him almost look like a ghost as he flitted down the dark corridor.

Candy was shocked to find her hands shaking as she poured out the coffee. After all, she had no responsibility. She could awaken Matron at any moment. She merely had to stay awake! The hot sweet coffee warmed her and revived her. She did another round and found Molly Broom sobbing, curled up into a round ball of tearsoaked misery. At first Molly resisted but then she gave way and clung to Candy, sobbing bitterly. It took Candy some time to quiet the child, and worried about the other patients. Candy wrapped Molly in a blanket and took her along to the Matron's room, there installing her in a chair, giving her some coffee.

After Molly was quiet and looked more herself, Candy said worriedly: 'I must just slip along and see if anyone wants anything, Molly. Stay here. You'll be all right.'

'I'm fine. I'll wait for you,' Molly promised, her eyes adoring Candy.

It took some time to make the rounds and she was dismayed by the time it had taken as she hurried back to the small room. She stood in the doorway and caught her breath with dismayed horror:

Molly had vanished . . .

In a blind panic of fear, she turned wildly, not knowing which way to look for Molly or where she could have gone . . . and she did not see the tall man walking down the corridor towards her until she bumped into him.

His hands steadied her. 'Candace — what's the matter?'

It was Dr. Faulkner!

The shock was too much. To her horror, Candy burst into tears. 'It's Molly,' she gasped. 'She's vanished.'

The tall, broad-shouldered man held the weeping girl close to his heart for a moment, patting her on the back. 'Molly is in bed,' he said. 'I found her half-asleep in the chair so carried her back to bed . . . '

'Oh dear . . . ' Candy hiccoughed

between sobs. 'And I was so afraid for her . . .'

Andrew Faulkner led her back to the small sittingroom, made her drink what was left of the now lukewarm coffee. Candy had stopped crying but the tears of fright still trembled on her long dark curly lashes and every now and then her mouth quivered.

'I'm sorry t-to be so silly,' she said. 'It is just that . . . that it was a bit eerie. I thought I was the only one awake and then . . . then Molly crying so bitterly and talking about her mother who hasn't written for a whole m-month . . . Molly thinks her mother may be ill and . . .'

'Her mother isn't ill,' Andrew said in a stern voice. 'She is just indifferent.'

The tears welled up again in Candy's eyes and she dabbed ineffectually at them with her hand. Andrew gave her his handkerchief. It had the faint scent of tobacco and as Candy dried her eyes, she thought how nicely masculine it smelled. At least she was calm again and could apologise once more.

'I think maybe I am a bit tired,' she confessed.

He looked at her strangely, perching on the edge of the table and frowning. 'I had no idea you were doing this. I worked late and met Kwido in the hall with the coffee. He told me who it was for . . . Whose idea was this?' he asked sternly.

Candy hesitated. She did not want to get anyone into trouble.

'Well . . . well, it seems they are very understaffed and so many children and staff have measles and . . . Nancy was very tired and so is Matron and . . . and both are on duty all day long and . . . Bill was a bit worried. I'm only doing this until two o'clock and . . . ' Candy said uncomfortably, wondering why he was staring at her like that. 'It was just that I thought Molly had . . . '

'Done something desperate?' Andrew asked gently. 'I think she's far too sensible. She has brains. That's partly

185

the trouble for she is intelligent enough to know that her mother can't be bothered with her.'

'How can a mother be like that?' Candy asked impulsively, and then regretted her hasty words for hadn't someone said there was a chance that Andrew might marry Mrs. Arden?

Andrew did not seem annoyed, instead he agreed. 'Some parents act strangely. I see it so often. They want to have children of whom they can boast — but they don't want to have to help them in any way. Not even by the simple method of loving them. Love is all important,' he said.

The world suddenly seemed very far away. There were just the two of them, sitting close together in the small pool of light thrown by the lamp.

'I think love is all important, don't you, Candace?' Andrew asked very softly.

She stared at him and caught her breath. 'Yes . . . yes, I do . . . ' she said quietly.

He leaned forward suddenly and cupped her chin in his warm hand and then — very gently — kissed her.

It was over in a moment and then he stood up.

'You're a sweet child, Candace,' he said almost sadly and left her.

She stared after him . . . and then she heard a child crying so she had to hurry to the bedside, pushing out of her mind the memory of that strange kiss.

In the morning, Dr. Faulkner stood by Candy's desk, his manner formal and his voice composed. Just as if nothing had happened. But something had — for everything now was different.

'I have to take Miss Stromberg into the hospital at Nsingisi,' he said stiffly, 'And I want you to accompany us.'

The rain still beat down out of a dark sky so Candy hurried to her room to slip on a thick white cardigan — it was always bitterly cold when it rained — and her macintosh. As she adjusted the tiny hat on her dark curls, she eyed herself thoughtfully. Now why were her eyes shining like that? Why had she this exciting breathlessness? To Andrew, she was simply a 'sweet child'. She must remember that. Then she realised that Andrew must have arranged this. Coming back from Nsingisi, they would be alone . . .

Her heart beating excitedly, she hurried down the stairs and to the waiting car. It was like a slap in the face to find Miss Rowland already installed in the seat by Andrew and to find herself relegated to the back with Miss Stromberg, whose massive beauty was shrouded in a thick blanket.

What a nightmare journey it was despite the chains on the car as the rain beat against the windscreen and the wipers seemed helpless. Andrew looked tense as he gripped the wheel. Although they travelled carefully, the car kept skidding on the steep mountain roads. Miss Stromberg grumbled unceasingly, blaming Matron for everything, including the *spots*.

It was a relief when they reached the

hospital and helped Miss Stromberg inside. Candy turned her head and saw Andrew driving off, with not even a backward glance for her. A little dismally she followed Miss Rowland down the corridor. Soon Miss Stromberg was in bed, clutching a hot water bottle to her heart and meekly letting the nurses take her temperature.

They left her in the small private ward and Miss Rowland said she had to see the Matron, if Candy did not mind waiting.

'I wonder if I might see Anthony Tester,' Candy said, feeling guilty because she had forgotten the sick man.

Matron, a tall woman with a tightly closed mouth, said that she could but she must not excite him.

Candy's high heels click-clacked down the polished corridor as she went to find Ward Three. The open doors to the wards showed her the beds were all occupied. Across the quadrangle from the African hospital came the wailing of babies, the crying of children and the loud voices of Africans as they chatted to one another.

Candy tapped on the half-open door and went in. She stood, transfixed with horror at the sight of the gaunt yellowish face with the skin drawn tautly over the high cheekbones. But Anthony's eyes were bright with surprised happiness when he saw her.

'How nice ... what a delightful surprise ... ' he whispered huskily. 'On such a dreadful day.'

She tried to hide her dismay as she took his thin cold hand and sat by his side. 'Bill told me you were here ... We've brought in one of the staff ... ' What did you talk about to a sick man? She took off the little macintosh hat and shook her damp curls. 'Matron said I mustn't excite you.'

Anthony looked amused. 'Matron doesn't know what she's talking about. I feel much better for just seeing you.'

She tried to make him laugh, telling him about Miss Stromberg's aversion to Matron, about little things at the school. She was distressed when his laugh ended in a painful hacking cough. 'I'm tiring you . . . ' she said unhappily.

He shook his head and clung to her hand. His eyes, deep-set in his face, frightened her a little by the intensity of their stare. 'Just to see you . . . you're so different from . . . all the girls I've known . . . ' he said quietly. He smiled at her. 'I wish I was ten years younger and . . . and healthy.'

She felt her cheeks glowing. 'Why, Anthony, what a sweet thing to say.' Her eyes smarted. 'But you are not so ill. You'll get better . . . '

He smiled at her and thin fingers tightened. 'Oh, yes, I'll get better and then I'll have another attack and so it will go on. Don't look like that, little Candy. I'm not afraid. You see I know that there is no death and where I am going I shall be well and happy. It is those who are left.' He half-closed his eyes for a moment. 'Dene. We are orphans. Alone in the world . . . ' He sighed. 'One gives one's life to God but shouldn't one think of one's sister . . . ' he said slowly. Then he smiled. 'I always forget . . . there's Bill. Of course Dene will be all . . . '

The Matron walked in at that moment and insisted that Candy should leave. She looked displeased at Candy who hurriedly bade Anthony farewell and promised to come again. Hurrying down the corridor in the wake of Matron's angrily swaying starched dress, they paused as a tall thin man in a white coat came hurtling down the corridor, his stethoscope flapping.

He skidded to a halt. 'Candy . . . ' He sounded pleased. 'Good girl. Seen Anthony?'

Bill took Candy's hands and swung them, smiling down at her.

'You're a good girl,' he said again. 'It means so much to Anthony.'

Candy was startled by his warmth.

Then she understood that any favour done to Anthony was a personal favour to Bill because he was Anthony's brother-in-law-to-be.

'He's a dear . . . I'm flattered that he likes me . . . ' Candy said.

'You may well be,' Bill said dryly. 'Anthony is hard to please.

Candy felt confused because Bill was staring at her strangely.

She laughed uneasily. 'I can't think why he should like me . . . I'm . . . '

'Can't you?' Bill asked. And then he said a very odd thing. 'I can . . . '

She felt so confused and bewildered by his strange expression that it was a relief to see Miss Rowland looking for her . . .

'Dr. Faulkner's here . . . ' Miss Rowland called.

Candy immediately forgot Bill, hardly noticing that he followed them out into the rain-drenched world. Candy was told to sit in the front this time and as the car drew away, she waved vaguely to Bill and then sat, staring ahead, very conscious that Andrew was by her side.

'We'll have coffee and sandwiches at the hotel,' Andrew said in his sternest voice, not looking at her. 'Then I am picking up two women who have been nurses in the past and who are coming to help us out over this emergency.'

Candy looked at his impassive face for a second. 'Matron will be relieved.'

She saw the smile make his mouth relax. 'And you will no longer be called upon to sit up at night . . . ' he said.

She felt her cheeks burning as she stared rigidly ahead, remembering every moment of that intimate little scene. Feeling the touch of his mouth on hers. She clenched her hands. Was he remembering it, too?

It was a relief when they reached the school and the two middle-aged plump women who were to help them out had to be taken to Matron and introduced, and their late lunch was a gay meal, no one noticing Candy's unusual silence.

Immediately afterwards, she hurried to her office and was grateful for the pile of work waiting for her.

Typing rapidly, she still could not get her thoughts under control. Why had Andrew kissed her? Was she making too much of an insignificant incident? Her cheeks burned suddenly with shame as she remembered that the previous secretary had fallen in love with Andrew and had been asked to leave as a result . . . Was she behaving in the same way? Would Andrew be embarrassed and upset if he knew? Did he really see her as a 'sweet child'? Didn't he realise that a girl of twenty-one was a *woman*?

When had she ceased to see Andrew as Dr. Faulkner and seen him instead as a man? And a very attractive man, too! At first she had been in awe of him, then she had relaxed because of his kindly friendliness; then surprised when he called her *Candace*, flattered when he told her she comforted him. When had her feelings changed to this hungry longing to have him take her in his arms?

'What exactly do you think you are doing, Miss White?' an icily angry voice asked.

With a start, Candy returned to her surroundings, finding Miss Faulkner by her side, gazing furiously at what Candy had typed. Still a little dazed, Candy stared at the paper in the typewriter and blinked as she read:

NOW IS THE TIME FOR ALL GOOD WOMEN TO COME TO THE AID OF CANDY.

11

Comfort

After days of torrential rain, the sun suddenly appeared, flooding the world with warmth and golden light. The wet ground miraculously dried up, great clouds of steam rising as the water evaporated. The grounds were pronounced fit to be used and the air was full of children's excited shouts and laughter. Almost overnight the tension that had filled the school and had afflicted Candy with a strange misery vanished. The last of the patients rapidly recovered and the two 'nurse-aides' returned to their homes in Nsingisi. As the sun blazed down out of a cloudless blue sky, Candy began to chatter and laugh again, telling herself she was over that odd illogical infatuation that had troubled her for a while. Now she saw Andrew as Dr. Faulkner again, a tall, impressive, rather aweinspiring man. A man who had been kind to her — a man she had nearly embarrassed by her stupidity.

Half-term came and an influx of parents, arriving in big cars to take their children out for the day. Candy drove some of the other children to Nsingisi to catch a bus that would take them to the railhead, for those who lived within reasonable distance were allowed to go home for the long week-end.

Molly Broom had begged for a lift to Nsingisi where she lived — she was *sure* her mother was at home. Miss Faulkner told Candy dourly, when Candy asked for permission to take Molly with her, that she was equally sure that Daphne Arden would be careful *not* to be at home.

'However, their house is not far off the main road and if Molly sees that her mother is not there, she may accept it,' Miss Faulkner said coldly.

'Molly is quite capable of running away which would put us to a great deal of trouble . . .'

Candy tried to hide her shock at the callous way of putting it. 'It seems rather sad . . .'

Miss Faulkner's mouth buttoned with disapproval. 'Many things are sad, Miss White, but we have to accept them. Unfortunately Molly seems unable to do so.'

Candy had two flags of indignant colour in her cheeks. 'She is very young to know that . . . that her mother doesn't love her.'

'Many of us have never known a mother's love,' Miss Faulkner said coldly, 'But we do not behave like juvenile delinquents. However, I understand she is behaving better these days. Also that she is very fond of you. Please do not encourage her, Miss White,' Miss Faulkner said harshly. 'We dislike what were once termed 'crushes' — they are unhealthy and hinder the child's progress.'

Candy bit her lip, fighting back an angry reply. But she was seething inside her as she drove a car load of excited children down the mountain roads, blessedly dry, now! Molly sat close to her, chattering excitedly. What was she supposed to do, Candy wondered. Snub Molly? Crushes were natural — just part of your adolescence. Why must Miss Faulkner always put the worst interpretation on innocent acts?

First they saw the bus-load of excited children off and then Molly told Candy the way to her home. Candy drove with a heavy heart and finally they came to a stop outside a small thatched house. All the windows were closed. Molly said quickly that her mother always shut the windows to keep out the heat — that it was the continental idea. There was dead silence as the car stopped. Not even a dog barking. The house was built under the shadow of the mountains and there was an ominous stillness.

Molly slid out of the car, the

excitement wiped off her face. 'I'll go and see . . . ' She walked a little way, then turned. 'You won't go without me?'

'Of course not,' Candy said and followed her. At the back of the house was a wretchedly neglected garden and a tall thin African woman with an arrogant nose and unfriendly eyes emerged from a tumble-down mud hut.

Molly spoke eagerly in the native dialect but Candy could hear from her disappointed voice that her mother was away.

Molly turned, her head drooping like a wilted flower. 'Mother is in Durban.'

What could one say? Candy thought fast.

'Rotten luck,' Candy said cheerfully, as if accepting it as the most natural thing in the world for a mother to go at half-term without letting her daughter know. 'Perhaps she had some business to do.'

'Business?' Molly said dully.

Candy led the way back to the car. 'Grown-up business. Solicitors, banks . . . all very boring,' she said.

Molly's eyes brightened. 'Yes, perhaps she had to go and she didn't want to . . . '

Candy starting the car went on improvising. 'I'm sure she didn't . . . she probably got a telegram at the last moment and couldn't let you know . . . '

By the time they reached the school again, Molly was laughing happily and even when the children gathered round her with broad grins and asked her where her mother was, Molly's eyes went on shining.

'She was called away to Durban on business. She had a telegram and rushed off,' she said proudly.

Candy was a little dismayed that her attempt to cheer up Molly was now accepted as the truth. But did it really matter? Anything was forgivable so long as Molly did not lose 'face'.

As she went indoors, Candy saw Dr.

Faulkner. Obviously waiting for her. She still had the funny little breathless feeling when she saw him.

'Mrs. Arden wasn't there?' he asked.

'No, she wasn't — ' Candy said curtly. Her nerves felt raw with misery. How could Molly's mother behave as she did?

'You're angry — ' Dr. Faulkner said.

Candy's eyes were moist as she looked up at this tall impressive man whom she knew only saw her as a child. 'She doesn't deserve to have a daughter,' she said angrily.

He smiled. She was vexed with herself. Now she was behaving like a child! 'Few of us deserve what we are given,' he said dryly.

She found courage suddenly. 'Your sister says I mustn't be nice to Molly.' Candy's eyes were rebellious. 'How can it hurt Molly if I let her see I am fond of her? Your sister says . . . '

Andrew Faulkner put his hand on her arm. A firm warm hand that

203

seemed to thrust a message through her body, causing her heart to beat faster.

'Take no notice of Constance,' he said quietly. 'She cannot understand. Molly needs you — don't deny her that comfort. Comfort . . . ' He repeated the word slowly. 'The Quakers sometimes name their daughters that. It is a good name. You should have been called *Comfort*, Candace.'

She stared up at him, startled by his voice. It was almost like a caress.

'Dr. Faulkner . . . I say, sir, please can we . . . ' A plump boy in his early teens came to stand by them, his face eager. Dr. Faulkner's hand fell away from Candy's arm. As he turned his voice was — as always — courteous. 'Can you — what, Jenkinson?' he asked.

Candy escaped to her room and stood in the middle of it, gazing out at the sun-kissed view of the ranges of mountains. Why had he spoken like that? Was it her imagination or . . .

It *was* her imagination, she told her flushed reflection in the mirror firmly. Just imagination.

Half-term over, school settled down into routine again but the sun shone continuously. Candy found herself avoiding being alone with Dr. Faulkner. Not that he seemed to seek her out. He was a strange man, and found him hard to understand. Kind, yet so impersonal — and then he would change, his eyes would meet hers across the room and she would be startled at the warmth in them, or his voice would change as he spoke to her, becoming gentle.

One morning she had slipped into Assembly for prayers and heard Dr. Faulkner announce that — depending on half-term tests' results — certain of the children would be allowed to go to the Game Reserve if they wished to do so . . .

As the hum of excited conversation swept through the hall, Candy caught her breath. Would Dr. Faulkner remember his half-promise to her?

Later that morning, Dr. Faulkner gave her a list of names to type. The door to Miss Faulkner's room was half-open and from where Candy sat, she could see Miss Faulkner bent over some papers on her desk.

'By the way, Miss White,' Dr. Faulkner said in his somewhat precise way, 'I know you have not been in Africa very long and I wondered if you would care to join the Game Reserve outing? Miss Boone is also coming and I am taking Mr. Robinson to help me keep order for the children are apt to get over-excited . . . '

Candy clasped her hands but she stilled the eager words on her tongue, very conscious that Miss Faulkner could hear every word. 'It is very good of you to give me the opportunity, sir,' she said demurely. 'I would like to accept it, very much indeed.'

'Good. I'll let you have all the details later . . . ' Dr. Faulkner said curtly but as he turned away he gave her a special smile.

A smile that set her heart beating fast again . . . a smile that made her look ahead and think of a week alone with Andrew. Not alone with *him* — but with more chances of being alone than they ever had at school.

Nancy was wildly thrilled with the news. 'Who's going with us?'

'Bob Robinson . . . ' Candy told her excitedly.

'Oh Bob . . . ' Nancy said in an odd voice.

Candy laughed. 'Would you have preferred Malcolm?' she teased. 'He could still have taken along his newspaper. Bob will be more fun.'

Nancy looked at her. 'You like Bob.'

'Of course. He's fun, and kind and . . . well, he's nice. Don't you think so?' Candy asked, a little surprised.

'I don't know,' Nancy said, turning away.

There was so much to discuss, to plan, to dream about but at last the great day arrived. They went in the school bus, Andrew driving with Candy sitting by his side. The children piled into the bus, talking excitedly and did not stop even when Miss Faulkner came out on to the steps to frown disapprovingly.

Andrew, Candy noticed, was chuckling as he waved farewell to his sister, let in the clutch and the bus slid forward. Candy turned and smiled at Nancy and Bob who were sitting at the back of the bus. She wondered why Nancy, usually so good-tempered, was looking sulky.

When she turned to look at Andrew, he was smiling at her.

'Poor Constance,' he said. 'She does miss so much. Sometimes I think she hates to hear people enjoying themselves. The children's noise doesn't worry you?'

Candy was startled. 'Of course not. Besides they'll settle down later.'

'Exactly — ' Andrew said triumphantly. 'But Constance would never see that. She would demand instant quietness.'

'But they are enjoying themselves . . .'

Candy said, puzzled by his excited voice.

He smiled down at her and something in his expression made her heart seem to skip a beat. 'We're going to enjoy ourselves, too — ' he asked, 'Aren't we, Comfort?'

12

Not Just a Dream

It was a long journey over the rough corrugated earth roads and Candy was constantly thrown against Andrew's broad shoulder. Then he would smile at her and she would smile back at him . . . How different he was, away from his sister, as he teased the children and chatted to Candy.

She was almost sorry when the journey came to an end and they reached the Game Reserve and made for the Rest Camp where they all unloaded. Candy gazed round curiously at the cone-shaped, thatched-roof huts which were grouped round a large central building. The children trooped into their respective rondawels to change into jeans and shorts and Candy and Nancy, sharing a small hut, chatted as they also changed into light leisure clothes.

'Ever been to a Reserve before?' Candy asked, stepping into her new lime-green jeans, tucking in the white shirt.

Nancy, pulling on scarlet jeans, looked up. 'Yes, several times but only when I was a child,' she said and laughed. 'I want to see if it is as wonderful as I think it is. You know how children are apt to build up something in their minds that has no real resemblance to life . . . ' Nancy paused, seeing Candy's startled look, and then she blushed. 'I'm quoting Bob,' Nancy admitted and looked a little uncomfortable.

Candy chuckled. She was brushing her hair with her usual quick impatient gestures. 'It didn't sound like you . . . ' Tying a green ribbon round her dark curls, she looked at Nancy. 'Isn't he . . . I mean, isn't Dr. Faulkner different on holiday?'

Nancy was scowling in the small

spotted mirror as she carefully outlined her mouth. 'He always is,' she said, 'when he can get away from that sister of his.'

There was just time for a brief run before the gates would be closed for the night and Dr. Faulkner gave them all a small pep talk as he gazed at their eager excited faces and at the cameras slung from the children's shoulders.

'I want you to remember that we are all here to enjoy ourselves so we mustn't be selfish and spoil someone else's pleasure . . . ' he said in his deep attractive voice. 'Obey orders instantly, and on no account, is anyone to get out of the bus. Understand?' he asked, with a sudden smile.

'Oh yes, sir . . . ' chorused many impatient voices.

As the bus drove slowly over the gravel roads, Candy looked round her interestedly at the small green bushes, the funny spreading little trees. Again she was by Andrew's side and he slowed up and pointed his hand and she gasped as her eyes suddenly found the almost hidden herd of graceful impala. Several lifted their heads to gaze at the bus, the sun shining on their dappled coats but then they lost interest and started grazing again, moving slowly. It was amazing how their natural camouflage hid them from the unwary eye. Candy could hear the whirr of cameras — and maybe the impala heard them also for suddenly they were jumping and leaping through the bush — some leaping so blindly that they collided in mid-air.

As Andrew drove on slowly they caught glimpses of zebra — then the tall head of a giraffe gazed at them curiously from over a tall bush. The giraffe strolled out to have a good look at them as the bus paused, and then — just like a fashion model — he slowly turned in a circle to give them a good view before he walked off with his odd jerky gait.

The time rushed by but they had a glimpse of buffalo and then saw the grey bulk of an elephant in the distance but it was time to go back to the camp.

That evening Candy found it very pleasant as they sat round the camp fire, eating grilled steak, drinking cup after cup of sweet hot coffee. The air was filled with the tang of smoke and the smell of cooking food and the chatter and laughter of many relaxed people, determined to enjoy themselves. The real holiday mood. After the children had been sent to bed and the younger ones tucked up, Bob and Andrew with Nancy and Candy sat and talked sleepily. A strange roar broke the stillness and then a kind of screaming laughter. Candy looked at Andrew and he told her that the first was a lion and the second a hyena. She shivered — not from fear — but because of the excitement that filled her. When they parted, Andrew gave her a *special* sort of smile; one that she lay in bed thinking about long after Nancy had fallen asleep.

Two blissful days of driving through the Reserve, catching glimpses of elephants, great grey monsters who flapped their ears and stamped across the road, lifting their feet oddly, the steam pouring off their huge bodies; of watching hippo in the pool, lazily yawning, looking like prehistoric monsters; of many giraffe — of quite a few lions, mostly dozing in the sunshine, and of course, wildebeeste, kudu, and buck galore.

It was their last night and Candy sat by the fire feeling miserable. Bob and Nancy seemed happy enough, they were playing a hilarious game of double patience. The children had gone to bed and many of the other groups were breaking up and going into their own rondawels for an early night.

'Come for a stroll?' Andrew Faulkner asked quietly.

Her heart leaping excitedly, Candy gave him her hand and he pulled her to her feet. It was pleasant walking in the warm dark night, looking at the glow of the camp fires, hearing soft music drifting from the rondawels the occasional cough-like roar of a lion, the sudden chattering of monkeys.

They had walked out of the lights and were standing in the shadow of a rondawel, looking back at the groups of people round the fires, the strange silhouettes they made.

'We don't need words, do we, Comfort darling?' Andrew said quietly, his hands on her arms as he turned her to look at him.

She gazed at the dim blur that was his face. 'I . . . ' she began. And know that it was a moment for truth. 'No, Andrew, we don't,' she said.

He caught her close and one hand tipped back her head as he bent to kiss her. It began as a gentle kiss but Candy's arms were suddenly round his neck and she was returning the kiss with a strange unusual passion. She had never felt like this before . . .

When he let her go, they stood, holding hands, saying nothing for a long moment and then Candy whispered: 'What will your sister say?'

Andrew lifted her hand and held it against his mouth. 'She will accept it,' he said softly.

And then he kissed her again. And again — and again. Long thrilling kisses that made the world rock round Candy while the stars seemed to be doing a fantastic dance.

At last he released her and said it was time for them to return — it would not do for Bob and Nancy to guess. 'We must plan, my darling,' he added softly.

'Plan?' she asked, startled. What was there to plan? They loved one another — what else was there to it. He swung her hand slowly and as they came into the lighted part of the camp, she saw that he was very troubled.

'What is it, Andrew?' she asked him.

There was an air of unreality about the whole scene. The black night — the great arc of a dark sky with the stars twinkling and shimmering, and the huge golden moon — the glow of the fires, the voices of the people — the cry of the hyena that must be prowling round outside the fence.

Andrew smiled at her. 'But nothing too big for us to solve, darling,' he told her, squeezing her hand and then releasing it. 'I'm just wondering how to hide it.'

She stared at him, feeling suddenly cold. 'Hide what?'

'Why, my love for you, of course,' he said slowly.

Her heart seemed to jerk. 'Have we got to hide it?' she asked him.

'Of course . . . ' He sounded surprised at such a question. 'How could we announce it in the middle of term? Everything would be disrupted. It is going to be a shock for Constance, in any case, but I would not dare risk telling her just now when we are so busy.' He looked down at her, his face puzzled. 'Surely you understand, Comfort?' He waited while she struggled to speak for the disappointment flooding her was absurdly heavy. 'We can be patient when we have so much to look forward to, can't we, darling?' he asked and there was a wistful note in his voice that eased her pain.

'Of course we can . . . ' she said quickly and tried to smile at him.

'Oh, Comfort . . . ' Andrew said and now his voice was despairing. 'Don't think it is because I don't love you — or because I don't want the world to know about us. It's Constance. I owe her so much — I have to think of her health . . . ' He sighed. 'If we could keep it a secret until the holidays, everything would be simplified . . . '

Candy could see Bob and Nancy standing up, yawning, looking round. In a few seconds, they would see her . . . in a few seconds, she would no longer be alone with Andrew. She turned to him impulsively.

'Of course I understand, Andrew, and I love you the more for thinking of Constance. It's just . . . just . . . '

Her voice wobbled a little. 'Just that I am wondering if I can hide it.'

They were walking very slowly, trying to drag out their last moments together. 'We must help one another,' he said.

And then Bob was greeting them and they were all talking naturally as if nothing had happened and at last, Candy could creep into bed, yawning a lot in order to discourage Nancy from talking.

As she lay there in the darkness, she wondered if it could be true. Andrew Faulkner, so good-looking, so well-known, so brilliant . . . loved her. Why? What could he see in her? She curled up into a ball of happiness as she remembered his answer to her question when she had asked him that.

'I love you because you are so sweet,' he said. 'Who could help but love you?'

She had said nervously: 'I hope your sister will . . . '

And then Andrew had kissed her again. 'Of course she will . . . ' he had said, a strange note in his voice. Was it a note of triumph? 'When she realises why we want to marry, she'll accept it,' he had added.

Candy stretched herself in the cool bed, glad of the blessed darkness. She went over and over the conversation again, savouring each moment anew, hearing Andrew's deep vibrant voice whispering words of love, talking of the future.

It was not easy in the morning to behave as if the world had not been turned upside down but Nancy did not seem to notice anything strange about her behaviour, and Candy was amazed how politely formal Andrew could become and yet his eyes remain so warm and full of love when he smiled at her.

Everyone was snappy, it seemed to her, the children quarrelling and moaning because their holiday was over, and Candy felt the same sense of desolation, as if they had all lost something that would never be regained. Fortunately there was plenty to do for they were making an early start because clouds gathering in the sky promised an early change of weather and Andrew said he did not want them to run into misty rain or a cloud-burst.

She sat by Andrew's side in the bus. He looked down at her with a smile. '*Parting is such sweet sorrow* . . . ' he said very quietly, and she knew that he felt as she did, that things would never be the same at the school, that they would have no opportunity to be alone, to reveal their love. 'How are we going to hide it — ' he asked quietly.

Candy looked at him and felt sure her love was shining in her eyes.

'I don't know,' she confessed.

The children were squabbling and shouting behind them. The sun had gone behind a great mass of dark clouds. Involuntarily Candy shivered.

Andrew turned his head. 'Less noise . . . ' he yelled.

There was instant silence. It length-ened uncomfortably, and then slowly, insidiously, the voices began again, first as whispers, then a little louder — and louder still.

Andrew shrugged. 'They can't help it and I feel just the same. It is as if something very lovely has come to an end.' He looked down at her and his voice was sharp with fear. 'It hasn't, has it, Comfort? You do still love me? You will marry me?'

She longed to throw her arms round him, to reassure him. As it was, she had to content herself with a smile. 'Of course I will, Andrew . . . ' she said warmly.

He smiled at her. 'I just wondered if it was all a wonderful dream,' he said.

She stared at him. How odd that he should be thinking the same as her.

13

The Wonderful Idea

It was almost as if Miss Faulkner sensed something, for after their return from the Game Reserve, she grew more and more difficult so that Candy found herself tempted to tell Andrew she could not stay there any more, that she must leave until they could tell Constance the truth. But then Andrew would give Candy a quick significant smile across a crowded room, or brush her hand lightly with his as he gave her some letters . . . there were so many small ways in which he reminded her that he loved her.

The sun shone from a cloudless blue sky but something had happened to the school. Or was she the one who had changed, Candy wondered. The children were in a strange mood, sullen, grumbling, fighting. Even the staff seemed to be affected and the staff-room was full of complaints.

'Miss Faulkner isn't making it any easier for us,' Malcolm Fenn said with a rueful smile. 'Have you heard the latest? The annual party to which we invite the other schools in the neighbourhood has been cancelled because Miss Faulkner says the children have been slacking and the tests' results were poor.' He sighed. 'Much as I admire her many good traits, I do feel that she is a bit difficult.'

Candy was startled for normally Malcolm said little, hiding always behind a newspaper.

Gabrielle Leroux tossed her head in agreement. 'She is a fanatic — that one,' she said scornfully. 'She should be teaching saints, not children. She is of a stupidity . . . ' she paused. 'She is angry because the older boys pay me the compliments. Is it not natural that they should so do? Are they not little men . . . ? They must learn the

225

politenesses some time . . . '

Horace Hyde, who was, according to Nancy, secretly in love with Miss Faulkner said mildly: 'I think she is right in one respect, Gabrielle. You are inclined to go to a young man's head.'

The French woman fluttered long dark lashes at him. ' 'Orace — that from you is a vairy great compleement. I thank you . . . ' she smiled at him.

'Why doesn't Faulkner put his foot down,' Patrick O'Shea said crossly. 'Sure and I know he's scared to death of the old harridan but . . . '

'Patrick — ' Horace said in a shocked voice, leaning forward to shake out his pipe.

'Sure and I'm sorry, Horace, but I'm livid, man, just livid,' Patrick said, lighting a cigarette with trembling hands. 'The latest is that I must segregate the riding classes. Sure and I'm asking you — what harm could the poor darlings be up to while they're on the back of a horse?' he demanded.

Candy felt acutely uncomfortable as she battled with desire to leap to Andrew's defence, to point out to the others what they should have seen — that Constance's health was a constant source of anxiety to Andrew, but she dared not speak, lest she betray their secret.

She slipped away quietly to the sanctuary of her bedroom and unpinned the engagement ring Andrew had given her. She always kept it pinned to her petticoat so that it touched her warm skin, reminding her by its very touch that Andrew loved her. She put the ring on her finger, holding out her hand so that the light caused the lovely solitaire diamond to sparkle. How she longed for the day when she could openly wear it — when she could face the others and have the right to defend Andrew. If only the end of the term would come . . .

She re-read her mother's letter, suddenly longing for her. Her mother said again and again how sorry she was that she had not been able to get up to see Candy. 'The work piles up, darling, now they want me to fit in an extra class. They are so eager to learn I just can't refuse . . . ' she had written. 'I only hope you are as happy as you say. Sometimes I wonder . . . '

Candy found her writing-case and wrote to her mother.

'Please don't worry about me, Mummy darling. Although Miss Faulkner is an old devil and finds fault the whole time, her brother is wonderful. Honestly I am very happy indeed. I have something very exciting to tell you but I'll tell you it in the holidays for it's a secret now. I can't wait to tell you — it's so wonderful . . . '

She hurried down into the hall to drop the letter in the post bag. She hated to have her mother the least bit worried about her. Passing an open classroom door she saw a group of children standing round a figure on the floor. It was Miss Rowland! Crumpled on the ground and unconscious.

Tom Snipe, one of the prefects had sent for Miss Matron, he told Candy.

'She just blacked out — ' he said worriedly. 'I didn't like to move her.'

'You did quite right,' Candy said with a warm reassuring smile as she bent to straighten the crumpled skirt. Miss Rowland would not like her knees to be showing like that — she was always so neat ... Candy felt the pulse. It was slow and Miss Rowland's face was drained of colour and her lips looked blue.

Looking up, Candy saw the children's scared faces. She smiled at them.

'Don't you think you should go back to your work?' she said gently. 'That is what Miss Rowland would wish, I'm sure. I'll stay with her.'

The children seemed to melt away into their desks but the room was very quiet as they bent over their books, now and then glancing back at Candy as she knelt by Miss Rowland, trying not to look worried. Suddenly Matron was there, murmuring something as she knelt by the prostrate body. She touched her starched bodice significantly and said quietly: 'She's had these turns before. I've sent for Bill but we can move her to her room . . . '

Candy could feel the hushed tension throughout the school and she was surprised at the number of children who stopped to enquire about Miss Rowland.

'Everyone loves her,' Candy said as she sat with Matron, waiting for Bill's report.

Matron sniffed. 'And so I should think. She's the one who keeps Miss Faulkner from acting like a fanatic. I know I shouldn't say such things but Miss Rowland softens Miss Faulkner's orders, tries to alter them, often persuades Miss Faulkner to change her mind. She's the only one in the school who has any influence over her — or sufficient courage to face up to her,' Matron said and turned away to give her nose a good blow.

Candy traced a pattern in the tablecloth, hiding her eyes from Matron's shrewd gaze. Had they always talked like this about Miss Faulkner? Or was it just that she was ultra-sensitive since she learned how much she loved Andrew? She longed to say it was not fair to say things like that — that Andrew was only concerned about his sister's health. It was unlike Matron to talk so . . .

Bill came into the room with a weary step. He smiled vaguely at Candy but she realised that he hardly saw her as he flopped into a chair, stretching out his long legs. 'I don't like it, Matron dear,' he said as he pulled out his cigarette case, for once forgetting to offer it round. 'She's all right for it was only slight but . . . ' He lit his cigarette and tossed the match out of the open window, giving a swift apologetic grimace at Matron. 'Sorry — forgot . . . Where was I? Oh yes, I say she must go to Durban and see a specialist. She says she can't be spared at this important part of the term.' He sat up and stubbed out the hardly smoked cigarette in the ash-tray. 'I say that's madness. If something isn't done soon, they won't have a Miss Rowland at all. I think I'll go and put the fear of death in the Duchess. I know Miss Rowland *is* essential here . . . but what she needs is a thorough overhaul and a good rest.' He stood up, looking thinner even than usual, his face tired as he rubbed his hand over it. Then he gave Matron instructions about Miss Rowland, and at the door he turned, for a moment his usual carefree self. 'Wish me luck — ' he said and was gone.

Matron stood up and emptied the ash-tray, straightened the tablecloth. 'Now there is another who is not scared of her highness,' she said. 'Bill puts health first — but I doubt if she will. Still, if anyone can persuade her, Bill can, that I'm sure. She has a soft spot for him, and do you know why?'

she asked Candy as she went to put the curtain straight for the breeze was blowing it. 'Because he stands up to her and she respects him for it!'

Candy nodded and made an excuse to escape from the room. It was getting very hard to remain silent while they insinuated that Andrew was afraid of his sister.

And it was, eventually, Andrew who persuaded his sister to let Miss Rowland go to Durban for two days later, after they had seen Miss Rowland, accompanied by Constance Faulkner, set off in the car, driven by the African chauffeur, that Andrew followed Candy into her office.

'I have some letters I want to dictate, Miss White,' he said formally and dutifully she followed him with her notebook and pencils.

Once they were alone, he kissed her and the world seemed to rock and only steadied as he let her go and smiled down at her. 'I'm afraid we must be careful for some people have a nasty habit of forgetting to knock at times. Sit down, Comfort . . . '

How she loved that word on his lips. Feeling ridiculously shaky at the knees, Candy obeyed and smiled at him, then she unpinned her ring, slipping it onto her finger, holding out her hand to admire it.

'I do so love my ring, Andrew,' she said quickly. 'It keeps me close to you when things are bad.'

He leaned forward, his handsome face concerned. 'And are they bad, darling? It won't be for long . . . ' He smiled suddenly: 'Wasn't I clever?' he asked. 'I killed two birds with one stone, to use a hoary phrase. I persuaded Constance that Miss Rowland *must* go to a specialist — and I also said one of us should go with her.' He chuckled. 'Constance thought it was more proper that she should go — which was just what I wanted. So now we can snatch some moments alone together.'

She smiled back rather uncertainly. How he reminded her of small Tim who had boasted triumphantly that a supposedly twisted ankle had got him off P.T. so that he could finish his comic.

Andrew got up to give her a cigarette. 'You had better make some notes so that if anyone comes in, it will look as if I have just been interrupted . . . '

Obediently she took down half a letter and then he relaxed in his chair, stretching out his legs, smiling at her as she relaxed in turn.

'Darling,' he began, 'Let's talk of our future. Are you sure you can bear to be a headmaster's wife? Have all these noisy brats round you all the time? Don't they drive you nearly mad with their noise and their stupidity?'

Candy laughed gaily. 'Of course not. I'm just afraid I won't make a very good headmaster's wife, Andrew.'

He looked at her and his eyes twinkled. 'Maybe you've got a few things to learn, Comfort, but you will — in time. Just to walk instead of run, not to look quite so enchantingly young and gay, to talk in a more dignified manner. I think you will be a perfect one . . . ' His eyes half-closed and his face was sober: 'If only I could build up this school a bit more. If only I could get hold of another director . . . '

Curled up in the chair, legs tucked under her, Candy glanced round the room, realising for the first time that one day she would call this her husband's study. Her husband! She looked at the handsome thoughtful man and wondered again why he loved her.

'Are directors so important?' she asked idly, thinking that she would have brighter curtains for the room, a new carpet perhaps as well.

'Of course directors are important,' Andrew said, sounding so shocked that she immediately gave him all her attention. 'Most important and for several reasons. First . . . ' He marked the reasons off on his fingers in turn. 'First, they invest money in the school — this means enlargements of buildings, added amenities. Parents appreciate this and this, in turn, means more children come to the school and we get more fees and greater prestige. Secondly, their names are important and often their names are enough. For instance, if a world-famous man is a director of a school, it shows that he approves of a school and that is a great help . . . '

'I see . . . ' Candy said very slowly. Somewhere at the back of her mind there was a tiny seed of an idea. 'You have several directors?'

Again Andrew marked them on his fingers. 'Kim Powell, famous name, famous lawyer — Sam Covington, a millionaire. Mrs. Gilda Grace, not only wealthy but with many friends. Her grandchild is here and she is always sending us pupils . . . '

'You haven't a doctor?' Candy asked and it was as if the seed was sprouting as she held her breath, waiting for his answer.

Andrew shook his head. 'Not yet,'

he said rather sadly. He leaned forward and as he talked, his face came alive, his voice eager. 'If I could build up the school, I could sell my share in it. I can't leave Constance until I know that I have built secure foundations for her future. But once I have left Constance, we can start our own school . . . ' He gazed at Candy who stared back, eyes wide with excitement as the seed of a thought rapidly grew. 'Think of it, Comfort — ' Andrew said in his deep thrilling voice. 'You and I — all alone.'

'Andrew — ' The words bubbled out of her mouth like lava from an erupting volcano. 'Couldn't we ask my mother to be a director?' She held her breath as she watched his face.

'You mean . . . ' Excitement lit up his face for a moment and then it died. 'I wonder if she would, Comfort,' he said slowly. 'It's quite a responsibility. She might not approve of the school . . . '

'I'm sure she would . . . ' Candy said eagerly, leaning forward to lay her small warm hand on his. 'Don't you want her, Andrew?' she asked, suddenly wondering if that was the reason for his hesitation.

His hand gripped hers. 'Want her . . . Why, it would be the answer to everything. Your mother is so wellknown, her approval would be a great help. But . . . but I wouldn't like to ask her to be . . . '

'But I could ask her . . . ' Candy interrupted excitedly. 'I'm sure Mummy would be willing . . . '

Footsteps sounded outside in the corridor and Candy snatched up her notebook, bending her head, hating the secrecy they had to observe.

Andrew began to dictate in a wooden voice but she could see how he had clenched his hands as if tense. The steps passed the door and both could relax and smile at one another in relief.

'Comfort . . . ' Andrew said softly, and the way he said it made it sound like a caress. 'How lucky I am to be loved by you.'

14

Either I am a Liar or . . .

One afternoon Candy was getting some work up to date. Andrew was in Nsingisi and Miss Faulkner still away in Durban with Miss Rowland. As Candy sat in front of her typewriter, she slipped on her engagement ring and held out her hand, turning it this way and that, to let the light make the diamond sparkle. She loved the ring, though occasionally she had wondered if the diamond wasn't a rather large one for her absurdly small hand.

'Whose ring is that . . . ?' Bill demanded.

Candy jumped. She had heard the door open. She stared at the tall thin doctor whose fair hair was ruffled and whose face wore a strange look. He

240

closed the door behind him and leant against it.

'I didn't know you were engaged . . . ' he said.

Candy's cheeks were bright red with guilt as she pulled off the ring.

'It's a secret, Bill. Promise you won't tell anyone,' she begged, her voice frightened.

'I won't tell anyone if you tell me why it is a secret — ' he told her sternly.

She was pinning the ring to the inside of her frock, hiding it, patting it so that she could feel its coldness against her warm flesh but for once it failed to encourage her. She felt sick with fright. Andrew would be furious.

She stood up her face appealing. 'Please, Bill — ' she told him desperately, 'It is a secret.'

He did not relax. 'Why is it a secret?' he asked sternly. 'Are you sure he isn't married . . . '

'Of course Andrew . . . ' she began indignantly and then stopped — her hand flying to her mouth like that of a guilty child, her grey eyes large and frightened.

'Andrew . . . ' Bill repeated slowly. He frowned. 'Andrew Faulkner?'

Candy lifted her chin defiantly. 'And why not?'

There was a strange look on Bill's face. 'What does Constance say?'

Candy's eyes wavered under his direct stare. 'She doesn't know yet. That's why it is a secret. Just until the holidays.' She moved to Bill's side, laid her hand on his arm appealingly. 'Please . . . please . . . Bill, you won't tell anyone?' she pleaded.

He smiled down at her. 'Don't get so het-up, Candy. Your secret is safe with me. I'm just puzzled about the secrecy, that's all.'

'Oh, Bill . . . ' she cried, feeling limp with relief as she flopped into the chair. 'You had me really scared for a moment. You see, she must not find out for Andrew says she is not strong and makes terribly emotional scenes and . . . and it could make her really ill. But in the holidays, we can break the news gently and by next term she will have accepted it . . . '

'You hope — ' Bill said dryly. He leant against the door, folding his arms, his face, for once, grave. 'Correct me if I've got it wrong, Candy. Andrew is worried about Constance's health?' He waited while Candy nodded. 'He is afraid she will have a nervous breakdown?' he asked.

'Yes — that's it,' Candy said eagerly, grateful for his understanding. 'It seems they had a frightful row about the children being allowed to rock and roll and Constance was ill afterwards. He doesn't want to risk another emotional scene . . . '

'He doesn't expect Constance to be very pleased then?' Bill offered her a cigarette.

She answered after he had lit it for her. 'You know how she is, Bill,' Candy said, a little puzzled by his tone. 'She is so jealous and possessive.

Then of course she is afraid he may walk out and leave her in the lurch for she is so dependent on him. Andrew feels under an obligation to her because she brought him up. He says he can't leave her until he has put the school on a firm foundation and her future is secure . . . ' Candy said with her usual quick eager way of talking, her small youthful face was very earnest as she added: 'Andrew is wonderful, Bill.' Her eyes were shining. 'He is so unselfish and thoughtful . . . '

'I see . . . ' Bill looked at the glowing tip of his cigarette. 'You are happy, Candy?'

She clasped her hands. 'Oh, Bill, you have no idea. It is wonderful — ' she told him earnestly.

He opened the door and smiled back at her. 'I'm glad, Candy. Don't worry, your secret is safe with me.'

After he had gone, she sat and stared at her typewriter blindly, feeling relief sweep over her. You could trust Bill. How awful had it been someone else.

How furious Andrew would have been — how difficult it would have been to explain her childish behaviour.

She had finished her work and was tidying the office when Bill poked his head round the door. 'Can you be free tomorrow?' he asked cheerfully. 'Anthony is home and I'm going to the Mission . . . '

'Is he home again?' Candy asked quickly. 'I meant to ask you but . . . '

'You had other things on your mind, eh?' Bill asked with a friendly smile. 'Yes, he is better though far from well. I'll pick you up at two o'clock. Okay?'

'Okay — ' she said happily.

It was never difficult to go out for an afternoon with Miss Faulkner away so Candy was waiting when Bill called for her the following day. It was very hot with an oppressive feeling in the air and despite the fact that they were up in the mountains, there was a strange stillness — the flowers drooped their heads almost sadly, even the leaves of the trees were still and the children's shouts on the playing fields seemed somehow subdued. Great cumulus clouds were piling up in the blue sky as if a storm might be near, so Candy had taken a thick white cardigan to slip over her buttercup-yellow frock. She had brushed her dark curls until they gleamed and tied them back with a yellow ribbon, and she looked even younger than usual as she hurried down the steps to meet Bill.

'Good girl — punctual . . . ' he said, leaning over and opening the door for her.

'Mummy says that punctuality is an important virtue — ' Candy said with a prim little smile and dancing eyes.

Bill, letting in the clutch, chuckled. 'This fabulous mother of yours that you are always quoting. When are we going to see her?'

Candy curled up on the seat by his side, relaxed as she always was with

Bill. 'It isn't her fault. Her programme of lecturing seems to expand all the time . . . '

As they drove along the steep mountain road with huge boulders on either side, stones from the gravel road were flung up by the tyres, making noisy *pings* as they hit the car. 'I'd like to meet her very much,' Bill said, his eyes intent on the blind corners ahead round which cars had an uncomfortable habit of hurtling. 'I've read several of her books. Basically I agree with her but there are one or two points . . . '

Candy laughed happily. 'Mummy will love to argue with you. She simply loathes people who fawn and keep saying: 'Oh I quite agree with you — ' when all the time, you know they don't . . . ' she said.

'Infuriating. I know the feeling,' Bill agreed cheerfully as he slowed up abruptly to allow a herd of goats to stroll across the road. 'By the way, does she know about Andrew?'

Candy looked at his face quickly but he was staring ahead. 'Not yet,' she admitted. 'I'm telling her when I see her. It isn't very easy to write about it . . . '

'Isn't it?' Bill asked.

Again Candy glanced at him sharply — was there a strange note in his voice. But after all, wasn't he right? Why wasn't it *easy* to write and tell her mother? She fidgeted uneasily. How she hated the necessary secrecy — it spoiled so much.

The car was gathering speed as they climbed. There were even larger boulders lying on the veld either side of the road, while stunted green bushes grew from between the crevices.

'I have several spastic children amongst my African patients,' Bill broke the silence to say. 'If your mother could spare the time when she comes, I'd be most grateful for her advice.'

Candy turned to him eagerly, grateful for the chance to get back on their old friendly footing. 'I'm sure she'd like to see them. She can always find time for everything,' she said quickly. 'I'll ask her.'

'Good.' Bill swung the wheel round sharply so that they could make a steep turn. 'Is your father dead?' he asked casually.

'I don't know . . . ' Candy confessed. She told him what she had told Andrew — that she had never liked to ask her mother questions because they seemed to upset her so much. 'But she isn't bitter . . . and she doesn't dislike men or anything like that,' Candy added. 'Mummy is a perfectionist and if you fail to achieve something, you always have the uncomfortable feeling of having let her down. The only time I regret not being a pianist, is when I think how proud she would have been of me.'

'I'm quite sure she would far rather see you happy,' Bill said. He turned his head and glanced down at her, his eyes narrowed. 'You *are* happy?' he asked bluntly, his hazel eyes concerned.

Candy lifted a radiant face. 'Terribly happy.'

He looked ahead again, his mouth tightening for a moment. 'You like living here? You won't mind being a headmaster's wife? Constance's sister-in-law?' he asked.

Candy laughed gaily, putting up her hands to her wildly blowing-about hair. 'Andrew's a wee bit worried about that but he says I'll soon learn to be more dignified. As for Constance, I'll be very kind to her and try not to upset her and in any case, later on, we hope . . . ' She stopped her impulsive tongue just in time, feeling her heart give a little jerk of dismay. She had nearly betrayed their most secret plan — that one day they would have a school of their own.

She was grateful for the fact that the Mission buildings loomed up so that she could change the subject naturally. 'Is Anthony really better?' she asked.

Bill shook his head. 'He should be in bed but . . . ' He shrugged unhappily.

'There's nothing we can do, Candy, so I suppose he might as well live the life he loves.'

They found Anthony sitting in a chair in the sunshine, a dozen African children around him, as he told them a story. His face brightened when he saw his visitors but Candy felt sick with misery as she saw the effort he had to make to stand up.

'This is good of you,' he said, beaming down at her as he held her hand. One of the *umfaans* came running with a chair for her. 'Do sit down. The sunshine today is so warming.'

Candy found it terribly hot ! Anthony found it cold? Wasn't that a sign of debility or something? She met Bill's concerned eyes and gave a half-smile and a little reassuring nod and then he went off to find Dene and to visit the patients.

Despite the glaring sunshine, it was pleasant sitting there with the valley before them and as Andrew talked of the weather and of his children, Candy fought to hide the horror she felt as she looked at the valiant skeleton of a man.

She was startled when he said gravely: 'Candy, when you visited me in hospital, I was under drugs and said . . . said many things I shouldn't have said. Did I offend you in any way?'

Candy stared in amazement. 'Offend me?' She felt her cheeks grow hot. 'Oh no, Anthony, you paid me the greatest compliment a man can pay a woman.'

It was his cheeks that were red, now. 'I was afraid . . . you see . . . you see Sister said I talked about you all that time?'

'Is that a crime?' Candy asked gaily, her eyes stinging.

He smiled at her with such sweetness that her throat felt taut. 'I hope not — for I'm sure it would only be nice things that I could say about you,' he told her gently.

Dene came towards them, her hand

tucked casually through Bill's arm. 'Hullo Candy,' she said in a friendly voice but her eyes were hostile.

Candy smiled back and wished she could tell Dene that there was no need to be jealous of her for she was in love with Andrew, not Bill. Dene looked tired and thin and rather unhappy; now she frowned as she glanced at her brother. 'Time for your rest, Anthony,' she said, her voice sharp.

Anthony's face was dismayed. 'But . . . ' he began but Bill spoke at the same time.

'We'll come again, old chap, but I'm afraid I must be off, now.'

As they drove away from the Mission, Candy looked at him. 'Were you really in such a hurry or were you concerned for Anthony?' she asked.

'I was in a hurry,' he told her sternly, 'And it does not really matter how tired Anthony gets any more. My one wish is for him to be happy. He loves you, you know,' Bill added almost casually.

Candy's cheeks were hot. 'I know,'

she said humbly, 'I only wish there was something I could do about it.'

'There isn't much,' Bill told her. 'Except see him now and then — and maybe you could think up an excuse to write to him. Send him some magazines or something.'

'I'll do that, Bill . . . ' Candy promised. It was little enough.

She noticed suddenly that they were on a new road — a narrow winding road that looked as if it was seldom used. Even more startled, she stared curiously at him as he drove off the road, bumping over the rough grass, and stopped the car under a huge overhanging rock, out of which grew a tree at a strange angle but that shaded the car from the sunshine. She gazed at the view before her — it was too wonderful for words — the distant valley shimmering in the heat below them. So many vivid startling colours — the blueness of the sky, the green trees, and the strange patchwork colours of the distant valley through which meandered the silver ribbon of a river.

Bill turned to face her after he had switched off the engine. She felt cold — why was he looking so grim? 'I must talk to you,' he said sternly.

She twisted on the seat, tucking her legs under her. a little scared by his voice. 'What's wrong, Bill?'

He offered her a cigarette and as he lit them both she saw with surprise that his hand was shaking. 'Nothing is *wrong* — ' he said slowly, 'And yet everything is wrong. Maybe I have no right to talk to you about it, Candy — maybe I should mind my own business but you . . . you are young and alone here and . . . and susceptible.' He paused and she saw that he was gazing at her anxiously. 'I know I'm walking in where angels would fear to tread but I must . . . ' He rubbed his hand over his face and she saw for a moment how tired and worried he was. 'If I didn't . . . didn't like you . . . '

Candy tried to lighten the heavy atmosphere. 'That's the usual preliminary to a lecture,' she said gaily. 'What have I done wrong now?'

'It is not what you have done . . . ' Bill said slowly as he stared ahead of his. His next question came as a surprise. 'Do you know anything about Andrew's childhood?'

Candy tensed and her eyes were wary. 'I know that he was left an orphan when he was four years old,' she began. 'And that Constance who was fourteen years older than he was, has brought him up . . . '

'That is the bare bones of the story,' Bill said. He began to rub his hand round and round the steering wheel as he talked. 'He was a very delicate child and sleeping with his parents when a drunk native murdered them both. Constance was in the next room and heard the screams and ran for help . . . When she and a neighbour got back, Andrew was . . . well, delirious, hysterical. He clung to Constance and

256

for nearly six years, would not let her out of his sight.' Bill recounted the dreadful story woodenly but the horror of it gripped Candy who was staring at him silently. 'He overcame his fear of being alone in time but he still occasionally gets nightmares. He will dream that he is covered with blood — the blood of his mother. They found him under her bed, you see. Terrified he had crawled there and his mother's blood . . . ' Bill paused. 'I'm sorry, Candy, but he is entirely dependent on his sister. It is not his fault but . . . '

She found her voice. 'He had his own school . . . '

Bill looked at her and she saw compassion in his eyes, 'Don't think I'm blaming the poor chap. I'm not. He tries to break away but each time he has to go back to her. She is his father, mother, guide, support, everything. He started this school against Constance's wishes for she disapproved of his friend. Andrew did it as a gesture of defiance, a sign of independence. Unfortunately the school failed. Constance had to rescue him. It made Andrew a hundred times more dependent on her.'

As some of the sick horror receded from Candy's mind, she began to think lucidly. This was a very different story from Andrew's . . .

She saw that Bill's knuckles were white as he gripped the steering wheel and stared ahead. 'I'm telling you this, Candy — ' he said harshly, 'Because as Andrew's medical adviser, I don't think he is a suitable husband for you. If . . . if I wasn't so anxious about you, I wouldn't have told you for Andrew has a right to keep the secret of his dependence on his sister to himself. He wants to break away from her but he needs someone to replace her in his life — someone to support him, to comfort him . . . ' Bill turned sharply for instinctively Candy had moved as Bill used the word *comfort*. 'Andrew is completely dependent on Constance,' Bill continued slowly. 'I have been battling for ages to get him to see a psychiatrist. If you do marry him, I suggest you persuade him to . . . '

'Of course I shall marry him,' Candy said stiffly, fighting the sick anger she felt, the fear that would not be denied.

Bill gave her a strange fleeting smile. 'Well, first, you must face some facts. First, he will never throw off Constance. She needs him as much as he needs her so she won't let him go — ever. Secondly, he dislikes children but relishes the power he feels over them. His sister bosses him so he bosses the children in turn. Thirdly he is a liar. He told you Constance was delicate. She is as strong as a horse. He has less influence over her than I have. I kept asking Constance to send Philippa Rowland to a specialist but she would not hear of it — it was only when I proved that it might be cheaper this way in the long run.' Watching Candy's face, Bill said bitterly. 'I bet Andrew told you that he had persuaded Constance.' He chuckled suddenly. 'Don't look like that, Candy — as if the end of the world has come,' he said, more lightly. 'You don't have to believe me if you don't want to — Andrew is neither mad nor wicked — he is just an unfortunate devil who was born weak and could never throw off the horror of that childhood scene. Constance has encouraged him to depend on her and he does try to fight her domination — in fact, he puts up a pretty convincing façade at times.' Bill started the engine and began to reverse off the grass. 'You can take your choice, Candy,' he said more cheerfully. 'Either Andrew is a liar — or I am.'

'Please take me back to the school — ' Candy said huskily.

Bill lifted one eyebrow. 'If that's how you want it, Candy. You don't believe me?'

She stared at him with hate in her eyes. 'I don't believe you,' she said loudly.

They did not speak until they reached the school. As she got out of the car, Candy said coldly. 'Thank you for taking me to see Anthony.'

Bill towered above her and grinned. 'What perfect manners your mother taught you,' he teased. 'Even when you want to cry, you are still polite.'

She lifted her head and glared up at him, horribly aware that tears were very near. 'I hate you, Bill Abbott,' she said quietly, and walked into the school.

15

The Welcome Visitor

Candy went straight to her bedroom, drew the curtains undressed and crawled into bed. Later, when Nancy looked in, Candy said in a voice muffled by the bed-clothes.

'I've got a terribly bad headache, Nancy. I don't want anything to eat but please don't tell Matron.'

Nancy looked puzzled, then smiled. 'Too much sun, probably. All right you're best left to yourself,' she said. 'I won't tell . . . '

As the door shut, Candy felt the tears pouring down her cheeks. She felt exhausted. As if she had been beaten. She ached all over. She did not know why she was crying because of course she did not believe a single word of the lies Bill had told. Andrew was not like that . . . Andrew was not weak . . . Andrew was not a liar . . .

She turned her head into the pillow and wept for something very lovely had been destroyed. Bill was a liar . . . Bill must be a liar . . .

Worn out from crying and thinking, she dozed and then awakened with a fresh shock of horror as she remembered. Now lying in the darkness, she went over the conversation again and again. Why should Bill have lied to her? What motive could he have. Jealous? Yet why? He was going to marry Dene and had never shown any romantic interest in Candy. Hatred? Yet why should he hate Andrew? Why make up such a ridiculous, fantastic story about a man like Andrew? How could Andrew be *weak*? How could . . .

Outside the curtained window thunder was rumbling and a wind tore round the school, howling like a banshee and occasionally a bright streak of lightning flashed through the drawn curtains. Hunching the bedclothes over her head, she realised that the headache she had invented had arrived. Her eyes stung, her head throbbed. She could not think properly. It could not be true. Everyone admired and respected Andrew. It was all lies . . .

And yet . . .

Yet she had known for some time that Andrew did not like children — it was their admiration and respect he played to get. Shocked at the thought, she examined it. It was true. Andrew played to the gallery — he would alter his voice when he spoke to the children, smile at them but the smile never reached his eyes . . .

Yet he was a fine man. How kind. Understanding about her fear of storms, humble as he confessed his fear of spiders. How considerate of Constance's health . . .

She caught her breath with dismay . . .

Surely Bill would not lie about that? Then why had Andrew lied about Constance's health? Had he sheltered behind that fabrication to hide his dread of scenes? Was that why he had postponed the announcement of their engagement?

Candy shut her eyes firmly. She would sleep. Everything was always better when the sun shone . . .

Oh, why couldn't life be simple and straightforward? As it had been in England. Why must she fall in love with a man battling with so much trouble?

She lay very still, shocked in frozen horror. So she believed Bill? In her heart she knew that she had always been aware that Bill would not lie. Well, as Bill said, poor Andrew, it was not his fault . . . Why must she feel this sick horror? Andrew called her 'Comfort' — and that was what she must be. A comfort to him. As soon as they were married, she would make him see a psychiatrist and they would get the whole thing cleared up . . .

At last she fell asleep and when she awoke in the morning, it was to a fresh sun-kissed world and a more serene heart. No longer did she hate Bill for the disillusionment; she knew it was meant well. As she dressed quickly, She reminded herself that Andrew needed her . . . He called her his Comfort — now she must be it.

After breakfast, she slipped into the back of the Hall for the Assembly and saw Andrew standing on the dais, looking impressive, his deep voice resonant as he read the beautiful words of the Bible.

The same man. Just the same. Tall, broad-shouldered, darkly handsome — with a sweet way of smiling, a movement of his graceful thin hands. A man people admired and respected . . .

What was it Bill had said? A convincing façade?

Suddenly she could not bear it and turned and hurried to her little office. She was tidying the drawers for everything else was up to date when Miss Faulkner walked in.

Startled, Candy stared at her. 'I didn't know you were back, Miss

Faulkner,' she said after she had greeted her politely.

Miss Faulkner, regal in a dark blue frock, looked annoyed. 'I am aware of that, Miss White,' she said coldly. 'How is it that you were well enough to go out yesterday afternoon but too sick to report to me when you returned?'

'I . . . ' Confused Candy realised that Nancy must have protected her by saying she was not well. 'I had a bad headache . . . '

'Did you inform Matron?' Miss Faulkner asked.

Candy's cheeks were hot. 'No — there was nothing she could do. I just wanted to lie quietly in a dark room . . . ' she said.

'It did not occur to you to enquire if I was back?' Miss Faulkner's voice was colder.

'I'm afraid it didn't. We didn't expect you until next week,' Candy said frankly.

'We?' Miss Faulkner's eyebrows were raised.

Candy's heart seemed to skip a beat. 'The staff . . . I mean . . . '

Miss Faulkner stared at her and then turned away. 'Bring your notebook. I have a lot of work for you,' she said severely and led the way into her room.

The familiar angry rebellion bubbled up inside Candy. Was it necessary for Miss Faulkner to be so rude. Nancy put it: *to treat you like dirt*. How would it be when Miss Faulkner was her sister-in-law? Would she ever be reconciled to her brother's engagement? Would she allow . . .

Candy hurried after Miss Faulkner, making herself behave meekly as she took down the rapid dictation, typed the letters and silently accepted reproofs for mistakes she had not made. She was suddenly very weary . . . tired of it all . . .

The days passed in a strange mixture of emotions — one moment, she felt almost unbearably sorry for Andrew, the next she had to fight the desire

to tell him to stand up to his sister
. . . Candy longed to be alone with
Andrew — and dreaded it the next
moment. Would she be able to keep
quiet? If she asked if the dreadful story
of his parents' death was true, he would
know she had been discussing him. He
would feel she was disloyal, did not
trust him. He might even discover
that Bill knew about the unofficial
engagement . . .

It was some time before she realised
that Andrew was avoiding her. Now
he dictated his letters on the tape
recorder — was always out of his study
when she took the letters to be signed
— she would find them later on her
desk. Why was he avoiding her? Was
he afraid that if his sister saw them
together, she would guess the truth?
Was he afraid he could not hide his
love for Candy?

Candy was sleeping badly, lying
awake for hours, trying to sort out
her troubled feelings. She was still in
love with Andrew . . .

But it was a different sort of love. That first thrilling breathless love ... that amazement that such a wonderful man could love her ... had gone. Now Andrew was more of a human being — and a rather pitiful one. Her sympathy for him had destroyed some part of her first love for him. Now she felt protective, afraid *for* him, no longer *of* him. His voice had lost its magic. She found herself watching him, seeing what Bill meant by *façade* ... admiring it but ... Found herself listening to the things he said and wondering what was the real truth.

Of course she was going to marry him. One day when they could break away from Constance, they would have their own school and then ...

She was standing in the staff-room one day, staring out of the window and thinking about Andrew, when Bob suddenly put his hand on her shoulder, making her jump.

'Penny?' he said cheerfully.

She tried to smile, suddenly realising

that these days Bob was always cheerful, always whistling or humming. 'My thoughts are not worth it, Bob. Why are you always so jolly these days?'

'Near the end of the term — it is in sight at last,' he said and smiled at her. 'And the prison doors will open.'

'Oh Bob — is school as bad as that?' she asked him, trying to smile.

His eyes were kind. 'Isn't it? You're not looking so well. They overworking you?'

She laughed. 'Slightly — '

She was glad then that someone else came into the room and she could slip away to her room quietly. No longer did she find it hard to walk instead of run — no longer did she want to tease or be teased, to joke; she just wanted to be alone, and when she was alone she wished she was not . . .

She did up a parcel of magazines for Dene and a book she thought Anthony might enjoy and wrote him a letter. Not long for what was there to say that would interest him?

She took the parcel to Matron and found her, for once, relaxed in an easy chair, gazing out of the window thoughtfully. She looked puzzled as Candy asked her to give the package to Dr. Abbott and ask him to pass it on to the Testers.

'But you'll be seeing Bill yourself . . . ' Matron said in a bewildered voice.

Candy's cheeks burned. 'I don't expect so,' she began and hastily changed it to: 'I might not for I'm not always in my office when he looks in and I do want Anthony to get this soon . . . '

'Have you quarrelled with Bill?' Matron asked bluntly.

Candy felt uncomfortable. 'Not exactly but . . . but we did have a few words and . . . and I'd rather not see him . . . ' And perhaps he doesn't want to see me, she thought suddenly, after all, she had called him a liar . . .

Matron stood up and put the package on a shelf. 'I'll give it to him,' she said and straightened the ornaments on the small cabinet, avoiding Candy's eyes as she added: 'He is very fond of you.' Her voice was kind. 'In fact, more than a bit fond, I would say.'

'Oh no, Matron,' Candy said quickly and without thought. 'He's going to marry Dene Tester.'

'Dene Tester?' Matron echoed, staring at her, puzzled. 'Whoever said so?'

Candy wished she had never mentioned it. It might be betraying a secret if she admitted that Anthony had told her. 'Everyone — ' she said vaguely.

'Then everyone is wrong — ' Matron said flatly.

A timid knock on the door interrupted them and when Matron turned to open it, it revealed Molly Broom, her hand on her swollen cheek, eyes huge and unhappy.

'Toothache again?' Matron said briskly. 'We'll have to fix a visit to the dentist, child, you can't go on like this . . . ' Her raised eyebrows as she glanced at Candy said their unexpressed thought — that it was Molly's mother's place to see the child visited the dentist regularly — but what a mother! 'Come along, Molly,' Matron said in a kind but firm voice. 'We'll fix it with some oil of cloves . . . ' She set off down the corridor for the small dispensary.

Molly hesitated, looking at Candy wistfully. 'Are you sick, too, Miss White?' she asked.

Startled, Candy said. 'No, I'm all right, thank you, Molly. Why?'

'Molly . . . ' Matron called impatiently. 'Do you want . . . '

Molly gave a wild glance down the corridor and then looked at Candy.

'Because you're so quiet and you never smile these days,' she said and bolted down the corridor like a scared rabbit.

Rather shaken, Candy went to her bedroom and took a good look in the mirror. What she saw shocked her. Huge eyes with dark shadows underneath them. A mouth that drooped dismally at the corners. Pale skin — lank hair that looked as if it hadn't been brushed properly for ages . . .

Which was the truth!

She picked up the brush and vigorously attacked her hair, brushing until her arm ached, knowing it would take more than one treatment to look the way it should. Carefully she made up her face. Forced herself to smile and then grimaced at her own reflection. It was absurd to betray your inner confusion and misery. Whatever happened Bill Abbott must not be allowed to see her looking so beaten.

She sat down abruptly on the edge of the bed.

Beaten!

The word described exactly how she felt.

Which was absurd because she was going to marry Andrew because she wanted to . . . because she loved him . . . because someone had to rescue him from his possessive sister, give him a chance to prove himself a man, able to stand alone. He called her his little Comfort . . . What was she doing about it? Had he noticed how miserable she was, creeping about as if all the joy had suddenly gone out of her life.

She must alter her appearance, force herself to be gay . . .

As part of her new plan, she went to the staff-room later that afternoon. She was going to be very gay, very cheerful. Whatever happened no one — least of all Bill Abbott — must guess how unhappy she was. As she walked into the room, she was met by a gale of laughter. A crowd seemed to be collected round a particular couple, laughing, and talking loudly. As she joined them, Candy saw that it was Nancy, and Bob Robinson, both looking flushed, both smiling at one another.

Horace turned and saw Candy. 'Just think, Candy. The school's pet wolf and our little Nancy . . . ' he said, beaming.

Candy kissed the radiant girl. 'How lovely, Nancy. I must have been blind. I never guessed . . . '

'Neither did anyone else,' Fabian said in a dry voice.

Candy turned to Bob. 'I hope you'll both be very happy . . . I'm sure you will be . . . ' she said, smiling at him.

He smiled back. 'We will be.'

When Candy could get Nancy alone for a second, she asked: 'When did it happen? You might have told me . . . '

Nancy blushed. 'It all happened so quickly. You see . . . you see I'll admit I've always liked Bob very much but I never thought he would look at me. Then . . . then . . . ' She smiled at Candy. 'He seemed to like you so much and . . . and I was a bit jealous. You always enjoyed being together and had so much to talk about and . . . ' She squeezed Candy's arm. 'Then Bob began to talk to me more and when we went to the Reserve you practically ignored him and . . . and you went out with Bill Abbott and . . . ' She laughed at Candy's startled look. 'I know I was silly but you are so pretty . . . well . . . well . . . this afternoon

277

we were talking and Bob said he had saved enough money and planned to give up teaching and try to paint for a living . . . and then he said he needed a model and how about me . . . and could I cook . . . and was I over twenty-one or must he go and ask my father for my hand in marriage . . . ' she giggled happily. 'I thought he was fooling . . . only then he kissed me and . . . and I knew he wasn't . . . ' Her face was radiant. 'But we wanted to keep it a secret for Miss Faulkner won't like it and . . . '

'What on earth has it got to do with her?' Candy demanded.

Nancy shrugged. 'She won't like it . . . '

There was no hope of keeping it a secret! All through dinner, Bob and Nancy were teased and both looked as if they were floating on a cloud of happiness. Candy slipped away early to bed, feeling strangely bleak. How she wished that she and Andrew could have looked like that; shy, confused, but so proud of their love.

Next day when Candy went to breakfast, she found Nancy looking very pale but with two bright flags of colour in her cheeks.

'We have to leave right away . . . ' Nancy told Candy, her voice shaking. 'Miss Faulkner said . . . said the most terrible things.' Nancy turned away but not before Candy had seen the tears in her eyes. 'And they're not true . . . ' Nancy said vigorously. 'Bob isn't a wolf . . . ' She rushed out of the room.

Matron told Candy what had happened. Nancy and Bob had planned to keep it quiet until the end of the term but someone had caught Bob kissing Nancy and had teased them and in the end, Bob had admitted that they were going to be married. 'All would have been well but someone . . . no names mentioned for I won't hold with gossip,' Matron said firmly, 'But as you know I never did like that German woman

279

nor trust her, either . . . but someone went to Miss Faulkner and told her and she sent for them late last evening and . . . ' Matron paused and shrugged. 'I don't know just what she said but she accused them of all sorts of things and sacked them on the spot . . . Bob is so angry . . . '

'But can she do that to them?' Candy cried, horrified. 'Isn't there a nicer way for them to leave. People might say all sorts of things . . . '

'Exactly — ' Matron said. She looked round to see if they were alone. 'You know, Candy, I don't like leaving a sinking ship but I am going to look for another post.'

'Matron . . . ' Candy gasped. She tried to picture the school without Matron, so strong, so reliable, so unfailingly cheerful and kind. 'Could . . . couldn't Dr. Faulkner persuade his sister to change her mind?

'Him!' Matron said with deep contempt. 'He's all hot air and talk and that's the pity of it. She needs someone with courage to face up to her.'

Unhappily Candy went down to her office. She would miss Nancy. Besides it wasn't a nice way for the girl to be dismissed.

Miss Faulkner called her into her room and did not tell her to sit down.

'Miss White — ' Miss Faulkner's voice cracked with ice. 'Did you know about this . . . this liaison with . . . Miss Boone and Mr. Robinson?'

Liaison? Miss Faulkner had used the word before. She must look it up in the dictionary, Candy thought, for it had such a . . . such an ominous unpleasant sound.

'I only heard of the engagement last night, Miss Faulkner,' she said stiffly, trying to keep a hold on her quick temper.

'You had no idea? Heard no talk?' Miss Faulkner persisted.

Candy drew a deep breath. 'I had no idea and that is the truth — ' she said firmly and glared at Miss Faulkner, who looked a bit startled and said in a surprisingly mild voice:

'That will be all, thank you, Miss White . . . '

Back in her own office, Candy looked up the word in the dictionary.

Liaison. Union or bond of union. Illicit union between a man and a woman . . . she read.

What a horrible word! She was on her feet, dictionary in hand, about to go in and tell Miss Faulkner she must not use such an ugly word in connection with Nancy and Bob when she heard a car draw up outside.

Automatically she moved to the window to see who it was and a woman got out of a big black car and looked up at the building. A tall thin woman with a shock of white hair and a tired anxious face which lit up with a smile as she saw Candy at the window.

'Mummy — ' Candy cried excitedly.

She forgot everything else, almost tumbling out of the front door into her mother's arms.

'Oh, Mummy — I'm so glad to see you . . . ' she said, and never before had she meant those words so much.

16

A Reason for Marriage

Even as Candy released her mother, she saw from her mother's face that they were not alone. Turning her head, Candy saw Miss Faulkner standing in the doorway, looking regal and consciously gracious.

'Is this your mother, Miss White?' Miss Faulkner said, showing her teeth in a wide smile as she came to greet them. 'Dr. Elisa White . . . ' Miss Faulkner said almost proudly. 'I am so pleased to meet you. My brother and I have been looking forward to this . . . '

Candy saw the very wary look in her mother's eyes, noticed the slight but instinctive withdrawal her mother had made even while she shook hands, and stifled a sigh. Miss Faulkner was her brother's worst enemy sometimes.

'Very nice of you to say so, Miss Faulkner,' Candy's mother said briskly. 'I had hoped there would be some hotel near here where I could stay for a few days.' She smiled ruefully. 'I had no idea you were so isolated.'

'Of course you must stay here,' Miss Faulkner insisted. 'Please come inside. Is this your car?' She gave a quick glance of appraisal at the black Jaguar and the smartly-clad African chauffeur waiting at attention.

Candy's mother laughed — a young amused laugh. 'My goodness no . . . ' she said. 'Our car is a wee thing in comparison and it is in England. This belongs to a friend of mine who has lent it to me for this trip.'

'The chauffeur can find accommodation in the location behind the school — ' Miss Faulkner said stiffly as if she was not amused. 'Please come inside . . . ' She gave a smile without warmth as she glanced at Candy, 'I think we can forget work while your mother is here,

Miss White — ' she said smoothly and turned to Candy's mother. 'Your daughter is the most efficient secretary we have ever had,' she said graciously, inclining her head slightly.

'I'm glad to hear that,' Dr. White said but from the tone of her voice Candy knew that her mother did not like Miss Faulkner.

The 'guest room' proved to be a pleasant suite of rooms: bedroom, sitting-room and bathroom. While Candy's mother washed the dust of the journey off her and changed into a simple severe white linen suit, she asked strayed questions and let drop odd comments.

'The school is bigger than I expected — ' she said as she dried her hands on the thick fluffy towel. She glanced round the beautifully furnished room. 'Plenty of money spent, I see . . . Is Dr. Faulkner away? Oh, I see — he teaches . . . M'm . . . '

At last she was ready, her white hair combed into some vague resemblance of neatness, her eyes shrewd as she came to sit by her daughter.

'Now, tell me, Candy . . . ' Dr. White said as she looked at the now quiet girl who sat so stiffly on the edge of her chair. 'Why did you write and tell me you were so wonderfully happy — and yet you look so miserable?'

Candy hesitated, looking at her mother's warm compassionate face with troubled eyes as she debated whether to tell her or not. It was so lovely to be together again, just as they had always been with life so uncomplicated and pleasant. Just to see her mother sitting there made her feel better — as if everything could be smoothed out. And then the words tumbled out of Candy's mouth. She would not have told her mother, risking her mother's impression of Miss Faulkner, but already Miss Faulkner with her sugary sweetness, her obvious fawning, had done the damage.

'Miss Faulkner's so *odd* . . . ' Candy said. She told her mother about Nancy and Bob, about Miss Faulkner's angry accusations, her insistence that they leave the school immediately. 'Just as if they had done something disgusting. It isn't fair . . . ' Candy said indignantly, her cheeks flushed. 'Nancy isn't like that — nor is Bob. They're both such nice people. You know how it is, Mummy. People will gossip so and things get exaggerated. Should Bob ever have to teach in a school again, this story might ruin his chances and . . . '

Her mother moved in her chair a little. Did she look relieved? What had she expected Candy to tell her? Dr. White's voice was mild as she spoke.

'I should think anyone knowing Miss Faulkner would immediately recognise the situation for what it is — simply an example of what can be caused by frustration. Miss Faulkner obviously has a mind that can only see the worst side of things. While professing to be shocked, she is inwardly delighted at having exposed what she calls 'sinfulness'.' Candy's mother smiled slightly. 'Do I sound very unkind? I meet with so many women like Miss Faulkner in life. Unfortunately marriage is not always the solution and many mothers are like that and it makes life very difficult for their unfortunate children. You must not let it upset you, Candy. I agree with you that it is unjust and unnecessary but this man Bob . . . ? Oh, Bob Robinson . . . he sounds an experienced man of the world and once his first anger has died down, he will find it merely amusing and rather pathetic. Is Miss Faulkner always difficult.'

Candy leant forward, clasping her hands, her face unhappy. 'Oh, she is Mummy. Her brother has a very difficult time. When I came she told me I must comport myself with dignity and not become involved in any romantic liaison with the staff. Liaison . . . it's a horrid word,' Candy added fiercely. 'I looked it up in the dictionary.'

Her mother's hand flew to her mouth. Candy wondered if it was to hide a smile. 'Candy, I'm sure the ordinary man in the street doesn't know the dictionary definition. It merely means an association, a romantic friendship, shall we say. I can quite understand that she could not have her staff falling in love and mooning all over the place.' Her eyes were shrewd now as she asked: '*You* aren't in love with this man, Bob?'

'Oh no,' Candy said fervently, her cheeks hot.

Her mother offered her a cigarette and they paused while she lighted them. Her mother leant back in the chair, looking at the wonderful panorama of beauty before the window as her gaze passed over mountain after blue mountain.

'A lovely view . . . ' she said dreamily. 'I take it Miss Faulkner is not easy to work for — I gathered from your startled look that the charm just now was obviously put on for my benefit.

Why, I don't know. I'm just a children's doctor. Poor by her standards.'

'And . . . ' Candy stopped herself in time. 'Her brother,' she went on, 'Thinks highly of you, Mummy.'

'How nice of him,' said her mother with a slightly rueful smile. 'Tell me about him. Hasn't he any influence . . . '

'He does his best, Mummy,' Candy said quickly, 'But his sister is . . . '

She paused. Dismayed. She had been going to say *delicate* — but Bill had said Miss Faulkner was as strong as a horse! 'She is very difficult — ' Candy finished and knew how weak it sounded, and that her mother had noticed the uneasy pause. 'She disapproves of rock and roll and . . . oh, there are lots of little stupid irritating things. Andrew doesn't agree with her methods . . . ' Candy talked swiftly, uncomfortably aware that she had called Andrew by his Christian name but knowing that it was too late to do anything about it, now.

'Andrew . . . ' her mother interrupted her, her face suddenly stern. 'Do you

291

call Dr. Faulkner *Andrew*?'

Candy swallowed and looked miserably at her mother. It had always been the same — she had never been able to hide anything from her mother.

'Yes,' she said and sighed. 'We're engaged, Mummy . . . ' As she spoke, Candy fumbled to undo the pin that kept her engagement ring pinned to her petticoat. 'Only it is a secret . . . ' she added, as she slipped the ring on her finger and held it out for her mother's inspection.

Candy's mother's face was expressionless as she surveyed the ring dutifully. She asked mildly: 'Why it is a secret?'

'Because . . . ' Candy began. Again she had to pause. Andrew had said it would upset Constance with the end of term tests so near and what not . . . but Bill had said that Andrew was scared to tell his sister. It *was* so difficult. Candy wriggled uncomfortably on the edge of the chair. 'We are telling his sister in the holidays, Mummy, because she doesn't like to mix work and . . . and pleasure.'

Her mother looked at her. 'Is she going to be pleased?'

They stared at one another for what seemed like an endless moment. Candy swallowed nervously. 'I'm afraid she isn't . . . ' She sought for the right words and began again slowly, staring down at her clasped hands, afraid lest her eyes betray her fear and uncertainty. 'You see, Andrew was four when his parents were . . . were murdered and Constance was eighteen and she . . . she took the place of his mother . . . and of his father, too, for she was all he had. I think she still looks on him as her child but he . . . he wants to break away from this school and start on his own. She doesn't want that. You see, she is a good organiser and handles the financial side but An — Andrew is the one who keeps the school together . . . ' Even as she spoke, Candy heard her voice dying away as she wondered if that was true. *Was* it

Andrew who kept the school together? Many little remarks overheard in the staff-room drifted into her mind now — was he such a good teacher — did the children really respect him — did the staff like him . . .

Candy's mother stubbed out her cigarette. Rose and found a fresh packet and silently they lit their cigarettes. Candy felt disturbed — this was a sure sign that her mother was worried, for otherwise she rarely smoked.

'I heard Miss Faulkner was very possessive, Candy . . . ' she said slowly. 'When Dr. Faulkner was at university, she lived in the nearby village and apparently he lived at home and went back immediately after lectures. He never took part in any of the extra-curricular activities — or in any games, nor did he join any club. I thought it was a great pity but imagined he might be in poor health. It seems more probable that his sister disapproved. I heard . . . ' she went on again, 'That he is a charming, well-educated man.'

A rush of relief flooded Candy. 'He is, Mummy. I — I couldn't believe it when he said he loved me. It seemed too wonderful to be true . . . and then,' she added, colouring as she spoke. 'He calls me Comfort,' she added shyly.

Her mother gave a small startled movement. Her face was concerned as she looked at Candy and suddenly she was stubbing out the newly lighted cigarette.

'So you are a comfort to him . . . ' she said, each word dropping slowly into the quietness. 'Is that what you want to be, Candy? A comfort to a man?'

Candy was grateful for the knock on the door that interrupted them. Seline, crisply smart in her starched blue frock and white apron, tiny white cap perched on black curls, handed a note. It was in Miss Faulkner's beautiful writing, asking Dr. White and her daughter to lunch with them in their own house.

'My brother is eager to make your

acquaintance,' Dr. White read aloud and looked at Candy. 'I wonder why . . . ' she added.

Candy's cheeks burned. 'Well — you are going to be his mother-in-law . . . ' she pointed out.

'H'm . . . ' her mother said and wrote a short acceptance and gave the note back to Seline. 'I suppose that could be the reason.' Almost instantly she changed the conversation and talked of her lectures and her experiences so that it was suddenly time to go to lunch and Candy felt nervous as they walked down the drive in the blazing sunshine and her mother admired the garden.

This would be the first time Candy had seen Andrew without a lot of people around them since Bill's devastating revelation. Her mouth dry, she wondered how she could keep Andrew from seeing that she had changed. That, though she still loved him, it was in a totally different way. How would Andrew treat her . . . would her mother keep the secret for her? She should have reminded her . . .

Candy's hands were damp with fear as they went into the small, beautiful house but Andrew greeted them with exactly the right amount of friendliness and deference, and included Candy in it, calling her *Candace* openly, making it plain that he liked her very much. It was a pleasant meal and a genial atmosphere and as they ate the perfectly served meal of crayfish salad, followed by cold duck, Candy glanced round her curiously. It was a well-furnished house but mentally she dubbed it as *ornate* — everything was just a little too elegant. The glass and silver gleamed, Johannes, the butler, was crackling in his starched white suit, his dark face a little sullen as he served them, there were the right sort of paintings on the walls. Everything was perfect — if you liked to live in a show-room.

Candy sat quietly for there was little occasion for her to talk for both Andrew and his sister were talking to her mother about her experiences in Africa, her opinions, her conclusions.

Afterwards Andrew showed them all over the school, behaving perfectly with just the right amount of modesty and pride, Candy noticed with a sick heart, for he was being like his house, a little too perfect. Once, when he had the chance and her mother was walking in front of them, Andrew gave Candy a quick significant smile, but most of the time he naturally devoted himself to her mother. He said he would arrange for her to dine with Candy in the staff dining-room and give her every opportunity to meet the staff.

'We are proud to have you visit us,' he said, bowing a little with a strange rather old-world grace to Dr. White. 'I will see you tomorrow . . . '

He left them to have tea with Matron and Mrs. Combie. The evening flashed by with Candy's mother seeming to enjoy meeting the staff, having long absorbing talks with each of them and when they went up to bed later, Candy saw from her mother's face that she was thoughtful and concerned, and deemed it a bad moment to discuss the important matter of a directorship with her.

After breakfast, Candy went straight to her mother's room, for Dr. White had gratefully accepted Mrs. Combie's suggestion of breakfast in bed.

Candy hurried into the room, smiling at her mother. 'Well, Mummy,' she said eagerly. 'What do you think of it? Wouldn't you like to be one of the directors?'

Her mother put down the piece of toast in her hand and stared at Candy, her face startled. 'Be a . . . a *what*, Candy?' she asked, amazed.

Candy sighed and could have kicked herself. She had never meant to ask her mother in that blunt way, she had planned to lead up to it gradually, but at breakfast, Matron remarked that Dr. White had said some very nice things about the school, and Mrs. Combie had said she thought Dr. White could help Miss Faulkner quite a lot if only the latter could be persuaded to listen, and Candy had had a wildly fantastic idea that once she and Andrew were married, they would persuade her mother to settle near them and help them with her advice. But now she saw that she had rushed things too much.

Curling up on the bottom of the bed, she eyed her mother warily, wondering what was the best approach.

'Now, Candy — ' her mother said sharply, her eyes anxious. 'What is this nonsense about being a director? A director of what . . . ?'

Feeling subdued, Candy explained. 'A director of the school. Andrew says it is very important to have the right names on the director's board. You see, as a well-known specialist on children, you would . . . '

'Vouch for the school?' her mother asked. She drank her coffee quickly and put the cup on the saucer with a little noisy plop. 'In other words, tell the world that I agree with the way the school is run — that I recommend it?' she asked in such a mild voice that for a moment, Candy thought her mother was going to agree. 'I couldn't do that, Candy,' her mother went on crisply. 'I disapprove strongly of the way the school is run,' she finished flatly and busied herself pouring out a fresh cup of coffee.

Candy stared at her mother's bent head and absorbed face with dismay.

'But you don't approve?' she almost wailed.

Her mother looked up and her face was stern. 'I most certainly do not. I like most of the staff, though not all of them. I like Matron and Mrs. Combie but I dislike Miss Faulkner and distrust her brother . . . '

'Mummy . . . ' Candy cried, sitting up stiffly, her eyes wide with dismay.

Her mother drank her coffee slowly and her voice softened as she went on. 'I am sorry, darling, if it is a disappointment but I must speak the truth. I do not approve of the way the school is run for there are undercurrents of resentment, I can see the children are not happy for they sense the atmosphere at once. The staff resent Miss Faulkner's autocratic manner, consider her unreliable, know she would never support them in any trouble that might crop up. They know that she is not the slightest bit interested in the children, only in their parents' cheque books . . . ' She paused and finished her coffee. 'You do see that I must refuse, Candy? Whose idea was it that I should be a director?' she asked mildly and then suddenly barked the question at Candy: 'Was it Dr. Faulkner's?'

Candy stared at her. 'It was my idea,' she began indignantly and paused. She was remembering the conversation with Andrew. It had been her idea but . . . but hadn't he rather paved the way for the thought by saying what a difference it could make to their future?'

She moved uneasily, sliding off the

bed. 'It was my idea,' she said stoutly. 'Then when I suggested it, Andrew jumped at it. He said it would help the school tremendously and then he could sell his share in it and we could start one on our own . . . '

'You'd prefer that?' her mother asked.

Candy twisted her hands together, her young face earnest. 'Of course. Oh, Mummy, Andrew has had such an unhappy life and he needs me . . . '

'Candy,' her mother said very slowly, 'Have you thought about this enough? You're only twenty-one and he is in his mid-thirties. You need a man you can lean on, a man who will look after you. If you marry this man, you will be the prop, the one to lead. He is weak . . . ' She paused and looked apologetic. 'I don't mean to be rude to him or unkind. He cannot help it, being dominated from such an early age by a strong character like his sister. Candy — are you sure you want to marry him?' Her eyes were concerned as she looked at her only child.

Candy shivered for a second. Was she sure? Then she heard a deep vibrant voice saying softly: *My Comfort — what would I do without you?*

She lifted her chin. 'Yes, I am sure — ' she said, and shivered again.

Her mother slid out of bed. 'Then I won't try to persuade you otherwise,' she said cheerfully. 'Now I'll have a quick bath and we can take the car and you can show me some of the beautiful countryside,' she said lightly.

Candy stared at her and was conscious of dismay. Yet she should have been delighted. She turned on the bath, watching the clouds of steam fill the bathroom.

'Mummy — ' she said unhappily as she went back into the bedroom. 'You couldn't change your mind about being a director?'

Her mother, busily creaming her face and wiping it with a tissue, an action that mildly surprised her daughter for normally she had no time for what she called 'beauty parlour business', looked startled.

'How can you ask me, Candy? It would be against my principles.' She stared at Candy thoughtfully. 'Candy — are you quite sure that is not the reason he wants to marry you?' she asked quietly and then slipped past Candy, and into the bathroom.

Candy felt frozen. She remembered that first interview. Andrew's amusement — the way he had teased her about her age — her certainty that she was too young to be given the job — Andrew's abrupt change of manner. His voice as he said thoughtfully. 'Dr. Elisa White? Is your mother Dr. Elisa White?'

Was it then that he decided to give her the post? Was it then that he planned to marry her if her mother would be a director?

If . . . ?

305

17

Did She Love Him Enough?

Candy was still standing in the middle of the room when her mother came out of the bathroom. She felt unable to move, to think clearly. Somehow she forced herself to turn and say lightly: 'I wish I could take you to see Bill.'

'Bill?' her mother said. 'Who is Bill — and why can't you?'

Candy sighed. 'Bill Abbott is the doctor here. He's young and supposed to be brilliant but . . . It's his mother who is a snag . . . '

Her mother was dressing with her usual quick movements. 'Have you quarrelled with him?'

Candy went to lean against the window, her head bent as she played with the tassels on the green curtain. 'Not exactly quarrelled,' she said in a troubled voice. 'But he told me something that I said was a lie . . . and now . . . ' Her voice tailed off.

Her mother brushed her mop of hair vigorously. 'Why can't we go there?'

'There's something queer about Bill's mother,' Candy explained as she looked up. 'They never entertain, she never goes out, no one ever sees her . . . '

Her mother gave a noise suspiciously like a snort. 'Probably because she finds the people here boring. People invent gossip — make mountains out of molehills,' she said scornfully, zipping up her linen skirt.

Candy's face was bright. 'I never thought of that — she may be just an eccentric.' Then her face clouded as she remembered. 'They say the Africans are terrified of her — they call her a white witch doctor . . . '

Her mother stared at her in dismay. 'Surely you don't believe such nonsense, Candy? I thought you had more sense.'

Candy laughed uneasily. 'I wouldn't

believe it in England, Mummy, but up here . . . '

'It'll be a good thing when the end of the term comes,' her mother said briskly, making up her face quickly. 'You need a complete change — most unhealthy atmosphere here. Now about this young man, Bill . . . '

'He wants to meet you,' Candy said, glad to change the subject. 'He has several spastic children amongst his African patients and he wanted your advice if you could spare the time. I said I knew you would. The trouble is, I don't like to drive us straight to his house. Without an invitation, I mean,' Candy said unhappily.

Her mother slipped on her linen coat and turned. 'Personally I would say the best thing we could do would be to drive there as if it was a normal household . . . ' she began and paused as she saw the distress on the young unhappy face. 'Telephone him, darling,' she added gently.

Candy looked at her watch. 'I might

just catch him — he has a surgery there early mornings . . . '

Bill was in! When he heard her voice on the telephone, he sounded delighted. 'It is good of your mother,' he said in his normal friendly voice, just as if the quarrel had never occurred. 'Now how can I . . . '

'My mother has a car here . . . '

'Good — that simplifies things,' Bill said crisply. 'Could she meet me in Nsingisi? At the hotel. I'll drive her to see my patients for it is a rough road to their homes. What time?'

Candy turned to ask her mother who was standing, waiting, a strange expression on her face.

'Any time, Candy,' she said. 'We could start right away . . . '

So it was arranged. But Bill had said ' . . . could *she* meet me . . . ' so Candy said she would stay behind, for they would want to talk shop and she would only be in the way. She said this all so eagerly and so earnestly but she still felt absurdly bereft and deserted when her mother accepted the suggestion and left her.

She was furiously attacking the pile of letters left on her desk by Miss Faulkner when Andrew walked in, his gown flapping. He came to stand by her side, his hands gripping her arms as he said in a hoarse whisper:

'I can't stop, darling, but how goes it?'

Her face stiffened as she managed a smile. 'All right . . . '

He gave her his usual brilliant smile but for once her heart did not seem to turn over.

'She does like me?' he asked and his eyes were bright and shining as she nodded and then he hurried out of the room again and Candy sat still, feeling sick with misery.

What had he meant? *How goes it?* was what he had said. Did he mean did mother like him as a prospective son-in-law . . . or was he thinking of the plan to ask her to be a director of the school.

Despite the hard work, her brain still whirled with unhappy thoughts. Her fingers flew over the keys but her mind was worrying over the problem. *Had* Andrew planned this all the time? Was Bill right and was Andrew terribly, frighteningly weak? So many little things came into her mind . . .

That rock and roll business. If Andrew approved, why must it be taken for granted that his sister has her way? It should have been a matter of principle — Andrew should have insisted. Constance's delicacy of which Andrew was always talking — her health — her emotional scenes. Not only Bill but Matron had many times, in Candy's hearing, talked of Miss Faulkner's lack of sympathy with the staff when they were ill, and had said it was due to the fact that she had never been ill herself.

It was a relief to escape from the tortured thoughts when her mother returned. Going eagerly to meet her, Candy noticed how grim her mother looked — and she was suddenly sure that Bill must have told her about Andrew . . .

As soon as they were alone in her mother's rooms, Candy could contain herself no longer. 'Bill told you about Andrew's nightmares,' she said accusingly. 'He had no right to . . . '

Her mother sat down rather suddenly on the bed, her hands on her squarely-planted, white sailor-shaped hat. 'What nightmares?' she asked bluntly.

Candy's hands flew to her own red cheeks. Why must she always blurt things out.

'What nightmares?' her mother asked. Taking off her coat, combing her hair, leading the way back to the beautifully-furnished sitting-room, sitting by the window. 'I had a most interesting morning,' she went on, leaning on the sill, gazing at the glorious view. 'He wanted me to stay to lunch but I wanted to get back to you for we haven't got so very long together . . . ' she added, almost wistfully.

Candy's throat tightened for she had been thinking that all the morning and wishing she had gone into Nsingisi with her mother.

'The holidays will soon be here. Then I'll be with you,' she said.

'But will you?' her mother asked. 'Haven't you got to break the news to Miss Faulkner?'

Candy's mouth was dry. 'I . . . I . . . '

Her mother glanced at her and then away again. 'Bill is a nice young man,' she said in a lighter tone. 'I rather wonder you didn't fall in love with *him*.'

'He's going to marry Dene Tester. She's a nurse, she lives at the Mission with her brother.'

'Is he?' Candy's mother sounded surprised. 'I got the impression that . . . '

'He's a confirmed bachelor?' Candy asked, with a little nervous laugh. 'So did I but . . . but Dene is nursing her brother who is slowly dying and . . . and . . . and so they can't think or talk of marriage at the moment.'

'I see . . . ' Her mother took out her cigarette case and offered Candy one. 'Now what is all this about nightmares?' she asked casually.

Candy looked at her in dismay. She had hoped her mother had forgotten the wretched word. Miserably she told her mother the whole story as Bill had told her, of Andrew's terrifying experience as a boy of four, of his dependence on Constance, his nightmares.

Her mother did not comment until Candy had finished, 'I see . . . ' She looked at her cigarette thoughtfully and changed the subject. 'Have you never wondered about your father, Candy?' she asked.

Startled and relieved by the way the subject of nightmares had been so easily accepted, Candy said: 'I've always wondered but it used to upset you so when I asked questions, so I stopped . . . '

Her mother smiled. 'Bless you — it did upset me. It still does if I let it but . . . ' She stubbed out her cigarette.

'I was a medical student when I met your father — so was he. That was how it began. I'm one of those lucky people with a photographic memory and I also absorb knowledge. Poor Lionel, your father, didn't, and I don't think he could ever forgive me for the fact that I sailed through the exams that he always failed.

'He was an only son and lived with his widowed mother. I loved him very much — ' Candy's mother was dreamy for a moment. 'So when he insisted we live with his mother, I agreed. I would have lived in a cave for him — ' she laughed sadly.

'It was some time before I discovered why we lived with his mother, I thought it was because she needed him. I learned that he was the one who needed her. He could never make any decision without asking her advice — he never stepped outside the house without telling her where he was going . . . '

She lighted another cigarette, her face sad. 'After a few years, I got restless. It had never worried me that his mother didn't like me, I was always busy and loved Lionel so that I accepted it. Then I discovered she was planting seeds of distrust in his mind . . . I was too friendly with the doctors — or I was neglecting him. He got very jealous and resented the fact that I soared ahead while he kept failing his exams.'

She sighed and flicked the ash off the cigarette end. 'It was a sad atmosphere and then she died in her sleep. I thought it might be a solution but it was the reverse.' For a moment, Candy saw her mother's face crumple in distress but then her mother recovered and continued: 'It was terrible to see a man go to pieces as he did. I moved us to a block of new flats — tried to rouse his interest. He stopped studying. I was qualified by then and working at a nearby hospital. He just sat at home, blaming me for everything. His failure to qualify — his mother's death — his unhappiness . . . ' Candy's mother put her hand to her mouth to hide it as it quivered.

'We had a terrible quarrel, Candy. I know it was wrong of me. I lost my temper. I told him to be a man, stand on his own feet or I would leave him. Of course I didn't mean it . . . ' She paused and swallowed.

'I had an urgent 'phone call in the middle of the quarrel. An emergency at the hospital. He — he begged me not to go. He needed me . . . I said it was my job, what kept us, that as a doctor I had no choice . . . '

She paused again and blew her nose, stubbing out her cigarette.

'When I came back, he was dead. He had jumped out of the window,' she said quietly.

Candy stared in horror at her mother. She longed to comfort her but what good were words?

'Your father wrote a letter before he died and posted it . . . yes, he *posted* it, to the coroner, saying I had driven him to his death. It was

all most ... most unpleasant ...'
she said slowly, looking at Candy and
suddenly smiling. 'And then I found
I was going to have you. I think you
saved my reason.'

'Darling Mummy,' Candy said,
knowing it was ineffectual. 'How
absolutely ghastly.'

Her mother smiled ruefully. 'I won't
say that it wasn't ghastly. It was. I still
wonder if I should have stayed. But
how could I? Someone was dying — so
I went, and someone else died.' She
passed her hand over her eyes. 'I knew
that it would have happened at some
other time — it was inevitable. He was
too weak — he had leant on his mother
for too long.' She leaned forward,
clasping her hands, giving Candy a
loving, searching look. 'Darling, I've
told you this because it looks as if
you are doing what I did. Loving
a man who is basically weak and
dependent on someone else. If you
wean him from his sister, he will
cling to you like a limpet — will

use you as a buffer between himself and every unpleasantness, just as your father did with me. If you ever try to throw off such an intolerable burden, he will blame you for everything, may even ruin your life as your father nearly ruined mine. You may not be as lucky as I was — you may not have a little Candace to comfort you . . . '

Candy began to speak but her mother stopped her. 'No, Candy darling, let me finish. I am not going to try to persuade you not to marry Andrew. If you truly love him, you will marry him whatever I say. But I do ask you to promise to be officially engaged — wear your ring openly and have everyone, including his sister, know of the engagement — for six months before you marry him . . . ' Candy knelt by her mother's side, holding her hands tightly, feeling strangely moved. 'Oh, I can promise that, Mummy.'

The gong boomed out noisily and Candy's mother sighed.

'We had better go down. I said we

would lunch with the children.'

They went downstairs to the clatter of young feet, the chatter and laughter. Sat at the senior table with Andrew smiling at them and the 'duchess' being very gracious as she made conversation.

Candy tasted nothing. Her mother's story had moved her. Could she face a life like that with Andrew? If she truly loved him, her mother had said.

The question was — did she?

18

No Way of Escape . . .

It was hard — harder than it had ever been in her life — to say good-bye to her mother this time, Candy found. Standing in the porch, with Andrew and Miss Faulkner witnessing their necessarily matter-of-fact parting, Candy ached with the longing to jump into the car by her mother's side, and be driven hundreds of miles away. Away from the confusion, the fear, the troubled thoughts.

But adults could not behave like that. Several times she had tried to talk again to her mother about Andrew, but her mother had been gently firm.

'Candy dear, you are an adult now and must work out your problems for yourself,' she had said quietly. 'If you love him enough to face all the difficulties that lie ahead, then you may be all right. This is something I cannot decide for you . . . '

Her mother turned from gazing for the last time at the wonderful view of the mountains, lightly kissed Candy's cheek, squeezing her hand tightly, and then politely shook hands with her host and hostess, got in the car and . . . was gone!

Candy felt as if she was all alone in the world as she watched the car vanish in a cloud of dust and then she followed Miss Faulkner's straight back into the school, and her heart sank and it was as if she was weeping inside her.

How had she got herself into this muddle? If ever there was a crazy mixed-up kid, she was one. Part of her was so achingly sorry for Andrew, so eager to help him build a new life — while another part of her was so terrified of the future that she wanted to run away as fast as she could.

'There is a lot of work to be done,'

Miss Faulkner said severely.

'Yes, Miss Faulkner,' Candy said meekly in a discouraged voice.

As the days passed and her nightmare sensation grew, it was as if the weather sympathised and wept with her, for the skies were packed with threatening clouds and there were frequent heavy showers. Candy had to work hard, but she welcomed it, falling into bed exhausted, grateful that she was too tired to think. She missed Nancy's young gay companionship very much; even the staff sitting-room seemed dull without Bob's cheerful jokes. She was always conscious that some time — some-how — Andrew would find a way of being alone with her, and then he would want to know what her mother had said. How would he react?

She had never felt so lonely or so unhappy in all her life before. She caught hasty glimpses of Bill Abbott, and he was just the same tall, good-looking, friendly man but she noted now that his eyes were impersonal, that warmth she had seen there before had now vanished. No doubt he felt he had done his duty by warning her but now had lost interest. She found herself avoiding the rest of the staff, keeping her head bent over her work if Andrew walked through the office, tensing herself nervously for the scene that lay ahead. Sometimes she was sure she loved Andrew enough to shoulder the burden — and then she would suddenly know with a sick horror that she could not face the sort of life her mother had led . . . she was not strong enough, she did not love him enough . . . But how could she tell him that? How could she hurt him . . .

She awoke one morning to a wet misty day and saw that the brightly-coloured flowers had bent under the night's heavy downpour. She had to go to the store-room for fresh stationery and knew that Miss Faulkner and Andrew were driving to Nsingisi so she looked forward to a tranquil morning without fear, so she was surprised when as she was typing Andrew walked into her office.

She stared at him, stiff and tense, and saw that he was not looking at her but at the notes in his hand as he said very formally: 'Miss White, when you have finished what you are doing, come along to my study. I have some notes to dictate . . . '

'Yes, sir,' Candy said meekly, knowing his voice was put on for the benefit of anyone who might be passing the open door. As she collected her things, she swallowed nervously. This was the moment she had dreaded. Yet why hadn't he gone with his sister? She knew that they had an appointment with Mrs. Grace and Mr. Covington, the millionaire director whose daughter had, Nancy had told her mischievously, been packed off to a finishing school in Switzerland because she was such a handful.

Her steps dragged as she went to Andrew's study and he was busy when she went in and merely told her curtly to sit down. She obeyed, looking at the windows against which the thick grey rain was beating. Today the study looked to her like a prison cell — cold and cheerless, the panelled walls bleak. She found she was trembling a little and she rubbed her cold hands together, looking at the absorbed face that had once been so dear to her . . .

It hadn't changed at all. The features were just as fine, the eyes as dark and compelling, the mouth curved just as gently, the hair was just as dark and thick, the shoulders as broad — but the magnetism seemed to have vanished. At least, it had vanished — for her

She was so intent on studying his face that it startled her when he suddenly looked up and smiled.

'Well . . . ?' he said and there was repressed excitement in his voice.

Candy swallowed. 'I thought — thought you'd gone to Nsingisi.'

He laughed. 'I was supposed to go but I convinced Constance that she could handle the directors better without my support. She loves to feel she can do without me, you know. Well, Comfort . . . ' he said and for once, the name left her feeling cold and afraid. 'Did you sound your mother out about becoming a director?'

The dreaded moment had come. Her mouth was dry. 'I'm . . . I'm sorry, Andrew, but she won't be a director . . . ' She clenched her hands fearfully.

He frowned, dark brows drawn together. 'She won't . . . ?' he echoed.

Candy swallowed. This would make it all right. Now he would not want to marry her and she would be free — free to escape from this nightmare . . .

'No, I'm afraid she won't,' Candy repeated.

She was startled when he rose, pulled her to her feet, and his voice was tender: 'Don't look as if the end of the world has come. I had little hope that your mother would agree. It was your idea . . . remember?'

'I'm sorry . . . ' she managed to say.

He put his arm round her and it was all she could do to stand still.

'Don't be. She will change her mind when she knows we want to get married . . . ' he said, pressing her head against his chest.

But I don't want her to change her mind . . . and I don't want to marry you, a voice seemed to scream inside her. For a moment, she thought she had spoken aloud. She closed her eyes tightly and stood passively as he tilted up her chin and stooped to kiss her. And as he kissed her, she knew the truth. That she could never — *never* marry him . . .

And then he released her and gently pushed her into her chair, glancing as he did so at the door nervously.

'We must make a fresh plan — ' he said gravely, going back to his chair and leaned forward.

Candy clutched the arms of her chair, forcing herself to smile in answer to his smile, searching for words with which to make him believe that she did not love him any more.

'Is it Constance?' he asked. 'Is it her methods?' He seemed satisfied when Candy nodded and he leant back in his chair, picking up his glasses from the desk, twirling them as he spoke. 'Never mind. We'll tell Constance in the holidays just the same . . . it won't make any difference to that.' He leaned forward suddenly, his face grave. 'Your mother didn't guess . . . about us?' He looked anxious for a moment so Candy shook her head, knowing it was cowardly to lie but lacking any courage at that moment. 'Good,' he said and smiled again. 'I'll come to Durban in the holidays with you. Maybe I could drive you there — we'll have to see what we can wangle . . . We'll tell your mother before we tell Constance, and I'll ask your mother about being a director . . . ' He was quite obviously thinking aloud, trying to find a way out of the difficulty, his forehead creased with lines, his mouth drooping.

She ached with pity for his disappointment. 'Andrew,' she said desperately, 'We must face it. Mummy says she has always refused to be a director of any school. She might always refuse. How could we break away from here?'

Andrew smiled. 'There are other famous people. Your mother must know many famous doctors, and you can meet them through her. If we look around we are sure to find one. A children's specialist would be best. I'm sure your mother must be friendly with one. You can keep your eyes open for me and . . . '

Candy seemed to sink into the chair. So it was to be up to her. Just as her mother had said: the onus, the responsibility would be hers. She would have to find a director — their chances of breaking with Constance would rest on her. If she failed, then the blame would be hers also . . .

A terrible weariness assailed her. Suddenly she felt too young for this situation. The sooner she got it over the better. 'Andrew . . . ' she began desperately. 'I'm sorry but I can't . . . '

The telephone bell shrilled. Impatiently. Imperatively.

Frowning a little, Andrew answered it. His face changed, he looked sullen. 'But Constance, I told you . . . I'm sure you can convince them . . . No, I don't want to . . . ' he spoke sulkily. 'What? Oh, is she?' His voice changed, brightened. 'I honestly don't think so, Constance . . . Oh, all right,' he said moodily, 'I'll drive in right away . . . '

Candy watched him, mesmerised with realisation of how right Bill had been. Andrew would always dance to the tune Constance called. She gave him one last compassionate glance and slipped out of the room and up to her own bedroom, where she could lock the door and stand, hands over eyes, as she realised that she still had not told him that she could not marry him.

As the days passed, she had no

opportunity to be alone with Andrew and it seemed to her as if he was avoiding her. He walked about with a strangely excited look on his face and sometimes she wondered how she would ever find the courage to tell him the truth and watch that jubilant look vanish.

Nothing Candy could do these days was right. Miss Faulkner seemed to go out of her way to make trouble and for once, Candy was all thumbs, making the most stupid mistakes, forgetting the shortest message. Fortunately the staff were engrossed with end of term exams. and no one paid much attention to Candy. One wet day she was typing, shivering despite the green cardigan she wore over her grey frock, thinking how chilly rainy days were in Africa, when Miss Faulkner came into the office, with a parcel.

'Miss White — I want you to take this to Nsingisi at once. Mrs. Grace is waiting for it,' she said in her usual arrogant voice.

Candy stared at her and then at the rain-drenched windows. 'But Miss Faulkner,' she began. She had been told again and again how tricky it was driving on these muddy mountain roads, how even an experienced driver could have a nasty accident as a result of a skid. Miss Faulkner waited, her eyes like marbles, as Candy struggled on. 'I've never driven in mud and . . .'

'Don't be childish, Miss White,' Miss Faulkner said acidly. 'There always has to be a first time. There are chains on the car and if you drive carefully, you should have no difficulty. This is urgent. You do know where Mrs. Grace lives?'

Candy swallowed. 'Yes but . . .' she began.

She was speaking to the air, for Miss Faulkner had put the parcel on the desk, and had vanished into her own room.

Candy stared at the closed door. Was Miss Faulkner trying to make her refuse to obey a command? Was this a trick? And then she looked at the rain. She had never driven in such weather. Days and days of heavy rain had turned the earth roads into quagmires. Andrew had told her . . .

She stood up. Andrew would not let her go . . .

She was half-way down the corridor when she paused. What would — or could — Andrew do? That frail reed would be helpless. Look at the other day, when he had meekly driven into Nsingisi simply because his sister told him to! No, asking Andrew for protection would only be humiliating for them both . . .

On her way to get ready, Candy paused at Mrs. Combie's room. But she was not there. Candy tried to find Matron, too, but she also seemed to have vanished. Candy hesitated. Perhaps Miss Faulkner was right, and she was making a fuss about nothing. After all, you could never learn to drive in mud unless you tried . . .

She changed into blue slacks and

a thick yellow pullover and then put her macintosh on top. One thing, she would be warm. The car had chains. She would take it slowly.

She hurried through the rain, sliding in the slushy mud of the path, to the garages, and the rain streamed off her macintosh and found its way down the back of her neck. It was a grey unpleasant day . . .

Matafeni, a garden-boy, was polishing the car in the garage.

'Where is Zacchary?' she asked the tall African who stood back as she got into the car. Zacchary was the chauffeur.

'He's very sick — ' Matafeni said, touching his stomach and bending over as if in pain.

That was her last hope gone so Candy carefully backed the car out of the garage. It felt strange with the heavy chains on the wheels. She drove very slowly, with her heart in her mouth, for the roads were steep and treacherous when wet, and she could remember the tense expression in Andrew's face when he had once driven her to Nsingisi in heavy rain. Gradually as the miles slipped by and nothing happened — and she found that she automatically corrected the small skids she had — some of the tension left her. But she had made her back ache by sitting upright so stiffly and she had to peer forward through the windscreen as the wipers worked valiantly — clack-clack, clack-clack, they went.

As she got nearer Nsingisi, the skies seemed to lighten and the rain slackened off. As she turned a U-turn, she could see the river below and that it was obviously in flood, tumbling and racing over the rocks, overflowing into the road either side. She slowed up — she would never get through the river. There was no room to turn — gingerly she tried to reverse and got into an instant skid so that plan had to be given up . . .

As she dropped nervously down the

steep road and the twists tortured the progress of the car, she wondered what she should do. Perhaps nearer the river there would be somewhere to turn . . . And then she reached a large sign that said *Detour* with an arrow pointing along a smaller road. With relief, she took this and found it was a longer way to Nsingisi but there was a high arched bridge crossing the swollen river and once past the bridge, she was in a valley and a watery sun came out and she saw that the road wound round the koppie where Bill lived.

The road ahead looked wide and smooth as if no traffic had passed over it recently but it was lined either side with high bush and turning a blind corner, she came on a herd of cattle. Standing in the middle of the road, their heads drooped miserably as they all huddled together as if to comfort one another — she was on them in a moment, there was not time to brake so she swerved to the side of the road and suddenly everything was taken out of her hands as the car spun round, flinging her from side to side of it — the last thing she was aware of was the car turning over, going off the side of the road, and then her head hit something hard and she knew no more . . .

19

How Foolish can you Be?

Vaguely Candy was aware of a cool hand on her wrist and a compassionate voice repeating again and again:

'You are all right. Your face wasn't touched. You are quite all right.'

Vaguely, too, she saw deep blue eyes and white hair.

Then she opened her eyes later and saw Bill's face — it was blurred and indistinct and she heard him say: 'You're all right, Candy girl.'

She kept floating off into black darkness, being spun round and round while her head throbbed painfully.

Once more she opened her eyes and saw her mother's grave, anxious face. 'You're all right, darling,' she said comfortingly.

Illogically perhaps, Candy felt cross.

Why keep on telling her she was *all right* when her aching body and throbbing head told her she wasn't? The walls seemed to billow towards her and away again and the bed seemed to be a boat on a wild sea, so she closed her eyes again and sank gratefully into sleep after she felt a gentle prick in her arm.

At last she awoke to a normal world and saw that she was in bed in a small room with palest grey walls and blue curtains, and as she moved a thin woman got up from a chair by the open window. Staring at her, Candy remembered vaguely the white hair and deep blue eyes.

'Where am I?' Candy asked. She moved gingerly, finding to her surprise that she could move and was all in one piece. But she kept yawning and was afraid she would fall asleep at any moment.

'I'm Bill's mother — ' the kind voice said. 'You remember Bill? The doctor . . . '

Candy yawned and half-closed her

eyes. 'But you can't be Bill's mother,' she said in the middle of another yawn. 'They call her a white . . . witch doctor and you're not that . . . ' Another yawn and her eyes were closed. 'You're nice . . . ' Candy murmured.

The next time she awoke she felt herself again and looked round with interest. Through the open window, she saw the sun shining and caught a glimpse of pink blossom against a blue sky.

'Hungry?' asked the little woman with the white hair.

Candy stared at her and remembered. 'You're Bill's mother . . . ?' she said in a surprised voice. 'I am hungry . . . ' she added, realising that she was. 'Am I really all right?' she added.

Mrs. Abbott turned away and in a moment returned with a mirror. Candy had not meant quite that but she gazed curiously at the little peaked face she saw reflected, the enormous shadowed grey eyes and rumpled dark hair.

'I told you your face wasn't

touched — that you were all right — '
Mrs. Abbott said, almost triumphantly.

'That was the first thing I heard,'
Candy told her.

'I'm so glad,' Mrs. Abbott replied,
beaming. 'It makes such a difference.'

Soon she brought in a tray of delicious
soup and then a light omelette.

Later Bill walked in, towering above
the bed as he took Candy's wrist in
his hand. His fair hair was ruffled. He
told her she had slight concussion and
severe bruising.

'It was very clever of you, Candy,' he
teased. 'Choosing to skid right outside
our gate. Mother was the first one on
the scene and she sent for me. We
decided not to move you. We were
a bit worried at one stage so we sent
for your mother. You remember?' he
asked, surprised, as she nodded her
head. He pulled a chair close to the
bed and straddled it, his good-looking
face perturbed. 'Tell me, Candy, what
made you take the car out on such a
day? You have had no experience of

342

driving on muddy roads and they were exceptionally bad.'

She wondered at the strange disturbed look in his eyes.

'Miss Faulkner told me to bring in a parcel for Mrs. Grace,' Candy told him.

He straightened the counterpane but did not meet her eyes. 'They found it. Miss Faulkner said she told you there was no hurry for it but that you must have driven off without her knowing anything about it. She is very vexed . . . '

Candy's cheeks flamed and she tried to sit up. 'She was the one who insisted. I was terrified. She told me there always had to be a first time . . . '

His hand was on her wrist but now he looked at her searchingly. 'Don't get excited — it isn't that important. It just seemed a daft sort of thing to do — driving in alone . . . '

Candy clung to his hand. 'We'll talk now. I tried to get out of it but she said I was being childish — that there were chains — that there had to be a first time . . . '

'And a last,' Bill said dryly. He was frowning still but she saw that he believed her. 'She was very angry because you pranged the car pretty badly. So I suppose she wanted the blame to be yours and not hers,' he said thoughtfully. 'Why didn't you go to Andrew?' he asked abruptly.

Candy stared at him. 'What good would that have been,' she said rather bitterly and saw the compassion in Bill's eyes and could not bear it. 'Has he been to see me?' she asked, thinking unhappily that the ordeal of telling Andrew that she could not marry him still lay ahead of her.

Bill looked uncomfortable. 'He sent some flowers . . . ' he said and there was a little silence, followed by Bill jumping up and saying that he really had no right to be sitting there, doing nothing. 'Oh, and Anthony sent flowers, also — ' Bill said, smiling from the doorway. 'He was on the telephone every day to know how you were getting on.'

As each day passed, Candy felt stronger but she was not allowed to get out of bed yet awhile. She grew to know and love the patient, loving Mrs. Abbott, who never ceased to surprise her and made her think that her mother had been right and Mrs. Abbott's strange behaviour was either eccentricity or a lack of desire to know the local people.

One day, Mrs. Abbott was sitting with her and they were drinking coffee when the older woman said suddenly: 'So they call me the white witch doctor, do they?' She sounded amused but Candy's face flamed as she looked in dismay at her companion.

'Did . . . did I tell you?' she gasped.

Mrs. Abbott chuckled. 'You were very dopey, my dear. Do they call me that because I don't mix with the outside world?' she asked.

Candy gulped down some coffee. 'It . . . it was the servants.'

Laughingly, Mrs. Abbott patted

345

Candy's hand. 'Candy you are an honest child,' she said. 'Look at me . . . ' Candy obeyed, mystified. Suddenly Mrs. Abbott was very grave. 'I want the truth, Candy. Does my face make you shrink away from me? Am I very hideous?'

Startled, and a bit frightened, Candy stared at the deep blue eyes, the amused gentle mouth, the white hair and saw for the first time that Mrs. Abbott's left cheek was marked with thin white scar lines.

'I never noticed your scars before — ' Candy said without thinking and then her hand flew to her mouth in swift dismay and her eyes widened with regret.

But Mrs. Abbott was smiling. 'Thank you for being honest.' Her face was radiant. 'You never noticed them?' Candy shook her head and Mrs. Abbott beamed. 'It just shows what a foolish old woman I have been . . . Wait . . . ' she said and hurried from the room, returning with a large album of photographs.

She propped it on the bed and slowly turned the pages so that Candy could see the lovely young face, vivacious — laughing — provocative.

'Myself — when young,' Mrs. Abbott said, her voice amused. She turned more pages and Candy watched the photographs change until now it was a beautiful, sophisticated elegant woman gazing up at her. 'Myself — when older . . . ' Mrs. Abbott added.

When Candy had seen all the photographs, Mrs. Abbott took the book away and came to sit by Candy's side, folding her hands, smiling.

'Candy — all my life I was a beauty. I was so proud of my face. You see, I was the only dunce in a family of six brilliant children and though my parents despaired of me often, they loved and were proud of my beauty,' she said, her face dreamy for a moment. 'I married a man who loved me for my beauty — and when he died, I used my beauty as a means of earning a living for myself and Bill. I used to demonstrate beauty preparations. All went well but not long after Bill qualified, I was in a car accident and when I recovered consciousness, I learned that I had lost my beauty. One side of my face was riddled with thick scars — they talked of plastic surgery but I would not listen. I wanted my old beauty back and that was something I would never get . . . '

She leaned forward and refilled Candy's cup. Thoughtfully, she added sugar. 'I wanted to die,' she said quietly. 'I had made a fetish of my beauty and life no longer seemed worth living. Bill was sweet to me. He came here to work to give me a chance to recover. He was sure that in time . . . in time I would feel differently.' Her face hardened. 'But I didn't. How could I have been so selfish, Candy? Spoiling his life. I couldn't bear anyone to look at me . . . I was like a child. I used to cover my face with a veil when I spoke to the servants . . . ' She chuckled. 'No wonder they were scared of me. I never thought of that. I was just a conceited old woman . . . ' she finished sadly.

Candy was staring at her in amazement. 'But Mrs. Abbott, honestly they hardly show and with good make-up . . . '

Mrs. Abbott sighed. 'I know, dear. I realise that now. Thank God you came along to cure me. You are the first woman — white woman — I have spoken to for years. I had to forget myself when you lay there, crumpled and unconscious. Afterwards, I believed you were half-doped . . . or else too polite to look at me properly.' She sighed again and went to the dressing-table, there to lean and gaze into the mirror. 'I haven't looked at myself for so long . . . I forgot that time heals all . . . ' She turned, her eyes bright with tears but she smiled. 'Thank you, Candy . . . ' she said and hurried from the room.

Candy relaxed in bed, surprised,

sympathetic, thinking of how good Bill had been to his mother, how understanding.

Next day Candy was allowed up and her legs felt absurdly shaky as Bill helped her to the sitting-room. She was very conscious of his arm around her — of his sympathetic help. But equally conscious that to Bill she was just a patient. As she gazed round at the antique furniture, beautifully polished, at the lovely old paintings on the cream walls, the blue curtains, she thought of the long time Mrs. Abbott had shut herself up inside these four walls simply because she could not bear to have people see that she was no longer beautiful ... It was hard to understand ... yet maybe if one was strikingly beautiful, it was as hard to lose that beauty as to lose a limb. Candy could not imagine it, for although she knew she was not *ugly* — no one had ever thought to call her a beauty.

How foolish can a woman be, Mrs.

Abbott had asked. Candy wondered miserably if the same words could apply to her. She should write to Andrew — it must be near the end of the term, now. Her mother had written to say that in a few days she would be sending the car for her, the car she was being still lent, apparently. Both her mother and Bill had decided Candy should go straight to Durban where her mother was likely to be for a short while. Candy wondered if it was her imagination or was it true that Bill was eager to get rid of her? He seemed to avoid her. Maybe it was Dene who was hostile — she had always shown it in her eyes even when she had appeared friendly. Maybe Dene was jealous — though she had no need to be. Bill certainly did not see her as a woman; why that day as he had helped her he had acted just as if he was putting his arm around a piece of wood!

Bill's mother came in with her quick light step, a wary look on her face. 'A letter for you, dear, from Miss Faulkner,' she said in a strange voice. 'Would you like me to . . . to stay . . . ?'

Candy smiled and tried to hide her surprise. Did she look so weak?

'I expect it is a scolding for being away so long,' she said lightly but as she turned the envelope over in her hands, she had a terrible fear that Andrew had told his sister and this letter was about them . . .

'Call me if you need me,' Mrs. Abbott said cryptically and vanished into the kitchen.

With a shiver of distaste, Candy slit open the envelope and pulled out the piece of paper. How thankful she would be when she was hundreds of miles away from the Faulkners, when she knew she need never see them again, when she had confessed the truth to Andrew and got that off her conscience. Would Miss Faulkner be furious when she gave in her notice? Suppose Andrew refused to release her, said he needed her, made a terrible scene?

'Owing to the extremely awkward situation your foolishness with the car has put us in,' Candy read. 'I have been forced to engage another secretary. An older woman and one far more suitable for the position so I have decided to retain her definitely. I shall not, therefore, be requiring your services any more and a cheque will be sent to you in settlement in due course . . . '

Candy lowered the letter and began to laugh. How typically Miss-Faulknerish! And she had thought Miss Faulkner would be angry if she gave notice! How blind can you be?

She had not finished the letter so she read on:

'I feel certain you will share our delight at the news that my brother

353

is to marry Miss Covington, the daughter of one of our directors. It should prove a most suitable marriage and will undoubtedly help considerably in the fulfilment of our plans for the school . . . '

Candy lowered the letter and stared down at it in amazement. A great wave of relief flooded her. She was free. Free. And then she was furious — disgusted with Andrew for his weakness, his cowardliness. Why hadn't *he* written to tell her? Had he asked his sister to break the news to her?

But the schoolgirl daughter . . . what was it Nancy had said? That the girl was 'wild' and had been sent away to a finishing school? Was it to see her that Andrew had been summoned to Nsingisi that day? The day that Constance insisted he joined her?

It didn't make sense. Andrew and a schoolgirl . . . Did they know one another . . . was Andrew so weak . . . and what about the 'wild' girl?

Surely she had spirit enough . . .

Mrs. Abbott came hurrying in with a tray of tea and some freshly-baked scones. She looked at Candy's face.

'She has upset you . . . ' Mrs. Abbott said accusingly. Candy blinked. She felt very strange. Somehow desolate. Unloved.

'She tells me Andrew is to marry the Covington girl . . . ' she said slowly.

Mrs. Abbott stared at her. 'But you knew . . . We thought that was why . . . ' She paused.

Candy caught her breath and her grey eyes widened. 'You didn't think . . . You mean . . . you don't mean you thought I tried to kill myself . . . ?'

Mrs. Abbott nodded and Candy began to laugh. 'But . . . but I *wanted* to be free . . . ' she said and suddenly the tears got mixed up with laughter and for a little while she could not speak.

Mrs. Abbott brought a horrible drink that she made Candy swallow and suddenly Candy felt better.

'Such a shock, you poor child,' Mrs. Abbott said as Candy leant back against the pillows in the chair, smiling weakly.

'But Mrs. Abbott, I don't *mind* . . . ' Candy said very earnestly. 'I had realised that I had made a mistake . . . ' She paused for she saw that Mrs. Abbott did not believe her, but thought she was being brave. 'What is the girl like?' Candy asked.

'A bit of a handful,' Mrs. Abbott said with a smile. 'Not a pretty girl — tall, skinny, blonde and not natural. I gather some time back, according to Bill, that she had quite a crush on Dr. Faulkner and her father was furious, said she was much too young and packed her off to Switzerland to this expensive school. I hear now that she eloped with a penniless artist and her father went after her and discovered that the man was married, so he brought Deb back with him, promptly got in touch with the Faulkners and they arranged everything.' She chuckled. 'Maybe Deb did it on purpose, I wouldn't know. I don't think Miss Faulkner will get things all her own way, though, for Deb is high-spirited and adores Andrew. They'll have plenty of money so maybe they will find happiness. I'm thinking that one day we may be saying: 'Poor Miss Faulkner'.'

20

Journey to Happiness

Her last day arrived and as the black Jaguar stood at the gate, Candy said good-bye to Bill and his mother. Candy felt horribly near tears and told herself it was purely weakness, but as she gazed at Bill's impersonal face, into his indifferent eyes, it was as if something died inside her. He was obviously impatient — had said he was going out to the Mission as he was worried about Anthony.

The telephone bell shrilled at that moment and as Candy hesitated, dragging out the moment of farewell for as long as she could, they could hear Bill's concerned voice. When he came back, his face was drained of colour.

'Anthony — ' he said curtly in answer to their inquiring looks. 'I

358

must go up. I've never heard Dene like that before. Quite hysterical.' He held Candy's hands for a moment tightly, gazing down into her tear-filled eyes. 'Don't grieve . . . ' he said gently. 'Anthony wouldn't have wished it. Remember, too, that everything gets better in time.' He touched his mother's shoulder lightly. 'May I bring Dene back with me?'

'Of course . . . ' she said and then he was gone.

Candy drew a long deep breath. So that was the end of that . . . She turned almost blindly to Mrs. Abbott and was enfolded in a motherly embrace. 'You must come and see us again,' Mrs. Abbott said, patting Candy on the back. 'Or I will come to Durban to see you.' Her face brightened. 'I'll do that, shall I?'

Candy's throat tightened as she kissed the older woman. 'That would be lovely. I'll write to you. I don't know what our plans are yet . . . ' she said and her eyes filled with tears. 'I don't want to go,' she said childishly.

'I know, dear . . . ' Mrs. Abbott said sympathetically. 'You have left your heart behind but . . . '

Candy turned on her almost fiercely. 'I do wish you would believe me. I stopped loving Andrew ages ago. Once Bill opened my eyes and I saw Andrew as he really was, I stopped loving him though I felt sorry for him.' She took a deep breath. 'You will ask Bill to give him that little parcel for me? It's the ring . . . ' She paused, remembering the pride and joy she had known when Andrew slipped it on her finger, and her constant sorrow because she had to hide it from the world's curious eyes.

Mrs. Abbott was staring at her strangely, 'Why, dear, I do believe you really mean it.'

'I do mean it,' Candy said again as they walked to the waiting car. 'I'm not saying I wasn't a bit upset because Andrew didn't tell me himself but knowing him, I can understand. And I know how I dreaded telling him that I wouldn't marry him . . . '

Mrs. Abbott closed the car door and looked through the window.

'What a pity it wasn't Bill you fell in love with,' she said wistfully. 'I'd have loved you for a daughter-in-law . . . '

Candy tried to smile. 'I think it is just as well I didn't for that wouldn't have been much good either,' she said wistfully. 'He's going to marry Dene . . . '

'Dene?' Mrs. Abbott cried. 'First I've heard of it. Did he tell you . . . ?'

Candy could have bitten out her tongue! 'No, it was something Anthony said. Thanks for everything . . . ' she added hastily and the chauffeur watching her face recognised that this was the moment to go.

'Good-bye . . . ' Mrs. Abbott called, waving and standing back as the car drew away.

Leaning out of the window and waving, Candy saw Mrs. Abbott's friendly loving face through a blur of tears and then she leant back in the corner of the car and kept her eyes closed, even as they drove through Nsingisi and all the beautiful mountains.

She was weeping inside her — and for many reasons. For this absurd weakness, this awful lassitude, this feeling that life wasn't worth living.

She wept for the fool she had made of herself, the stupid dreams she had woven, for her infatuation for Andrew. She wept for Anthony — for Dene ... But most of all she wept for herself — for she had nothing and no one.

She had got over the first awful misery by the time they reached Durban but when she saw her mother waiting for her, the wretched tears returned.

'It's lovely to see you, darling,' her mother began but her voice changed as she said: 'Very tired?'

'I do feel a bit tired,' Candy confessed. It was the coward's way out but she dreaded the thought of loving questions.

In an incredibly short time Candy was in bed, dutifully swallowing some tablets her mother gave her and finally she slipped into a deep blessed sleep.

When she awoke, she felt better. Still the empty desolation inside her but now she felt she had control of her stupid desire to cry. She went to the window and gazed at the blue Indian Ocean, at the still-empty sands, the palm trees waving in the slight breeze. She turned as the door opened and her mother came in.

'Mummy — I'm sorry I was so difficult yesterday . . . ' Candy said going to hug her mother.

'Darling, I could see how tired you were . . . ' Her mother said, kissing her warmly. 'And heartsore?' she asked gently for Candy had written to tell her that she had known she could never marry Andrew, she did not love him enough, and that he was going to marry Deborah Covington.

Candy shook her head. 'No. Just

relieved. There's so much to tell you . . . '

'And I've so much to tell you, too . . . ' her mother said.

There was a strange note in her mother's voice and Candy stared at her and watched the lovely colour flood her mother's usually pale cheeks, saw the shy uncertainty replace the composed look in her eyes.

'You're going to be married — ' Candy said.

Her mother gasped. 'How did you guess?'

'You look — different,' Candy said.

And then they were laughing and crying a little, hugging one another. Just like the old days — only quite different.

Later they talked. Over breakfast, Candy's mother told her about the American doctor she had met so frequently and got to know so well since she had been in South Africa.

'He is kind and . . . and very nice,' Candy's mother said shyly. 'I do hope you will like him,' she added anxiously.

'I'm sure I will — if he's nice to you,' Candy said stoutly but her heart sank a little. Everything would be different now. Even if she hated him, her mother must never know. Her mother deserved some happiness in life. 'You really love him, Mummy?'

'Oh, Candy — ' was all her mother could say, but after looking at that radiant face Candy knew it was more than enough.

They talked of Andrew's engagement. 'I was so relieved,' Candy confessed. 'I thought about what you had said and I realised I did not love him enough. I dreaded telling him and then . . . then it wasn't necessary. He just ignored me and got engaged to this wealthy girl.' Her eyes downcast, she played with her fork, twirling it round and round. 'I know it is silly of me,' she said. 'but I feel humiliated . . . sort of cast-off . . . if you know what I mean. I gave him my love and he didn't want it. All he was looking for was a new director for the school . . . and a wealthy wife . . . '

Her mother looked concerned. 'Love is never wasted, Candy. You gave him the gracious gift of your love and you could not do more. I think he would have liked to marry you but . . . but when I refused to be a director, he realised he could never get his sister to accept it. I'm afraid it was my fault . . . ' she said.

Candy stared at her. 'Then I must thank you, Mummy. I do realise I could never have stood life with him. I want a man I can trust — rely on . . . ' Her face clouded as she thought of Bill — and envied Dene. 'But there does seem an awful emptiness in my life . . . '

Her mother looked at her worriedly and then at her watch. 'Oh dear, I do wish I hadn't to leave you this first day but I've a lecture . . . ' She stood up and looked down at Candy with concern. 'Look, Silas is coming to dinner tonight to meet you. I hope you don't mind . . . '

Candy stood up and hugged her mother. 'Mind? I'm longing to meet him,' she lied gaily. 'What does he think of having a grown-up step-daughter?'

'He's thrilled to bits. He's a bachelor and has always wanted children. He wants us to go to California with him but we'll discuss that tonight . . . '

When her mother had gone, Candy wandered round the room aimlessly. She was delighted for her mother . . . it would be wonderful for her mother . . . but all the same Candy felt out of it. Desolate. No one needed her. What would California be like? And Silas? Whatever happened, she must make him like her . . .

Desperately she wandered along the Parade, looking at the crowded beaches, hearing laughter, voices; everyone else was happy. She looked at the great white luxury hotels — at the huge cars and she ached with longing for the quietly beautiful mountains.

Returning to the hotel, she saw that

Silas' car — for it was he who had loaned the car to her mother, she had learned — was parked outside and the chauffeur saluted her. Her mother had suggested that if she was bored, she went for a run in the car — out to the Valley of a Thousand Hills, perhaps — and suddenly weary of her own company, Candy told the chauffeur she would want him in ten minutes.

Inside the hotel she decided she would leave a note in her room for her mother in case she came back early. Passing through the crowded reception hall, Candy ached with the longing to get away from it all. There was no holiday spirit about her — just an overwhelming depression. Somehow she must shake off the misery and be bright and cheerful that night — Silas must not think he had got a miserable specimen of a step-daughter . . .

'Miss White . . . Miss White . . . ' the receptionist came running after her breathlessly. 'Telegram for you.'

Who would be sending her a telegram, Candy wondered, as she ripped it open.

Her heart seemed to stand still as she read the words:

'Bill hurt Love Lavinia White.

For a moment she felt she could not breathe — then she was hurrying to the lift — being wafted up seven floors to her room. She had forgotten her key but an African girl was cleaning the room so Candy could walk in. With a shaking hand, she scribbled a note.

'I have taken the car back to Nsingisi, Mummy. Forgive me but Bill is very ill.'

She found a coat and almost fled from the room and down in the lift. Fortunately she had money in her handbag for petrol . . .

But the chauffeur told her the tank was full. He showed no sign of surprise on his impassive dark face as she told him to take her back to Nsingisi and the house from which he had collected her.

It seemed an endless journey as

she sat bolt upright, tense and coldly, staring blindly ahead. Bill hurt. How badly was he hurt? It must be grave for his mother to have wired. If only she had given details . . . And why wire Candy? Dene would be there . . . But supposing there had been a car accident and Dene killed . . .

'Can't you go faster . . . ' She leaned forward to say to the chauffeur.

He showed surprise but obediently put his foot down on the accelerator and the car shot ahead. Even so, it still seemed an endless journey.

The almost unbearable agony of waiting taught her the truth. It was Bill she loved. Bill she must have always loved, even without knowing it. Bill — for with him she had always been at ease, happy. She had relied on him. Trusted him. Why hadn't she guessed the truth when she believed Bill in preference to Andrew? That should have told her . . .

At last Nsingisi came into view and they dashed through the small town with a scattering of barking dogs and a few heads turning from the hotel stoep but Candy doubted if anyone recognised her at that speed, and if they did, what did it matter? All that mattered now was Bill . . .

Almost before the car stopped, she was out and stumbling down the path to the front door. Supposing she was too late . . .

The front door was ajar — this frightened her still more. She hurried inside — going to the sitting-room to find Mrs. Abbott first . . .

Opening the door, she stood dead still, staring.

At Bill . . .

At a Bill who looked every bit as startled as she felt, as he clumsily got to his feet and she saw that one of his ankles was bandaged.

Without stopping to think, Candy burst into tears and rushed forward.

'You're all right and I thought you were dead . . . ' she cried.

She was in his arms, clinging to

him, and he was holding her close, saying over and over again: 'Darling . . . darling . . . darling.'

Her wet cheek against his, she tried to explain. 'Your mother sent me a telegram. She said you were hurt . . . '

'I was — in a way . . . ' he said and his voice was tender.

'I sprained my ankle . . . '

She gazed at him, tears balancing precariously on her long dark lashes. 'I thought you were dead — dying . . . '

'Would it have mattered so much?' he asked gently.

'Oh, Bill . . . ' She looked at him and it was all she could say. And then she remembered Dene, and was horrified. 'Dene — ' she said and tried to push him away from her.

'What about her?' he asked, holding her tightly. 'She's at the Mission clearing up the papers before she leaves . . . '

'But . . . ' Candy stared at him in amazement. 'You're going to marry her . . . '

'Are you quite mad?' Bill asked. 'Who said I was?'

She stared at him as she told him. 'Anthony told me you would take care of her and . . . '

Bill was laughing. 'That doesn't mean marrying her . . . ' he said and held her close to him. 'I've got her a job with a new clinic on some important project in Rhodesia — something that she will enjoy . . . ' He sobered and looked down at Candy's face. 'I was never in love with Dene, Candy. Surely you knew that it was always you I loved . . . '

She stared at him, her eyes widening. 'You gave no sign . . . '

He grinned ruefully. 'You could only see Andrew . . . '

'I was a fool . . . ' she said slowly, looking back at the past, amazed at herself.

A gentle sound at the door made them turn. Bill's mother was standing there, looking a little anxious.

'I'm sorry I frightened you so,

Candy . . . ' she began.

Candy slipped out of Bill's arms and went to hug Mrs. Abbott.

'You did frighten me . . . ' she said warmly, 'and I had a frantic journey here, expecting the worst . . . but it was worth it.' Her face radiant, she smiled at the older woman. 'What made you do it?'

Mrs. Abbott chuckled. 'I saw plainly when you left yesterday that we were wrong and it was not Andrew you loved, but Bill . . . and then you had said that Bill was going to marry Dene — and I *knew* that Bill was in love with you . . . ' she said a little breathlessly, 'And it all seemed so hopeless — two people in love but too blind to see it and both so proud and so . . . and so when Bill sprained his ankle, it seemed like an answer to my problem, for I could honestly wire and say he was hurt and . . . and I knew that if you loved him as much as I thought you did . . . '

'I would come back?' Candy finished

for her, laughing. 'And I did.'

'Yes — ' Mrs. Abbott said triumphantly. 'I knew that was the only way to convince Bill that you were not still in love with Andrew . . . '

Candy pushed her hair out of her eyes with a quick gesture and turned to Bill with a smile. 'He's convinced now, I think . . . '

'I most certainly am . . . ' he said and limped towards her while his mother slid quietly out of the room, closing the door after her.

Bill took Candy in his arms and murmured against her soft responsive mouth. 'I must be the luckiest man in the world . . . '

'And I am the luckiest woman,' Candy agreed fervently.

And then he kissed her and she knew that all her dreams had come true.

Other titles in the Linford Romance Library

SAVAGE PARADISE
Sheila Belshaw

For four years, Diana Hamilton had dreamed of returning to Luangwa Valley in Zambia. Now she was back — and, after a close encounter with a rhino — was receiving a lecture from a tall, khaki-clad man on the dangers of going into the bush alone!

PAST BETRAYALS
Giulia Gray

As soon as Jon realized that Julia had fallen in love with him, he broke off their relationship and returned to work in the Middle East. When Jon's best friend, Danny, proposed a marriage of friendship, Julia accepted. Then Jon returned and Julia discovered her love for him remained unchanged.

PRETTY MAIDS ALL IN A ROW
Rose Meadows

The six beautiful daughters of George III of England dreamt of handsome princes coming to claim them, but the King always found some excuse to reject proposals of marriage. This is the story of what befell the Princesses as they began to seek lovers at their father's court, leaving behind rumours of secret marriages and illegitimate children.

THE GOLDEN GIRL
Paula Lindsay

Sarah had everything — wealth, social background, great beauty and magnetic charm. Her heart was ruled by love and compassion for the less fortunate in life. Yet, when one man's happiness was at stake, she failed him — and herself.

A DREAM OF HER OWN
Barbara Best

A stranger gently kisses Sarah Danbury at her Betrothal Ball. Little does she realise that she is to meet this mysterious man again in very different circumstances.

HOSTAGE OF LOVE
Nara Lake

From the moment pretty Emma Tregear, the only child of a Van Diemen's Land magnate, met Philip Despard, she was desperately in love. Unfortunately, handsome Philip was a convict on parole.

THE ROAD TO BENDOUR
Joyce Eaglestone

Mary Mackenzie had lived a sheltered life on the family farm in Scotland. When she took a job in the city she was soon in a romantic maze from which only she could find the way out.